A
HOUSE
NOT
HER OWN

stories from Beirut

Emily Nasrallah

TRANSLATED FROM THE ARABIC
BY THURAYA KHALIL-KHOURI

gynergy books

COPYRIGHT © Emily Nasrallah, 1992

TRANSLATION COPYRIGHT © Thuraya Khalil-Khouri, 1992

ISBN 0-921881-19-3

Originally published in Arabic by Nau Fal Group

Edited by Lynn Henry

Cover Art by Jamelie Hassan

Cover Photo by John Tamblyn

Cover & Book Design by Catherine Matthews

Printed & Bound in Canada by

Imprimerie d'Éditions Marquis Ltée

gynergy books

P.O. Box 2023

Charlottetown, Prince Edward Island

Canada C1A 7N7

CANADIAN CATALOGUING IN PUBLICATION DATA

Nasrallah, Emily, 1931–
A house not her own
ISBN 0-921881-19-3
I. Title.
PJ7852.A56H68 1992   892'.736   C92-098533-5

TRANSLATOR'S NOTE

The short story is a relatively new addition to modern Arabic literature. It is only in the past three or four decades that it has grown to maturity.

Most Arabic literature is written in the classical Arabic language, a unifying language among all Arab nations, understood by all Arabs from the Atlantic to the Mediterranean to the Persian Gulf. Colloquial Arabic, on the other hand, differs from one Arab country to another and, at times, from one region of the same country to the other.

Emily Nasrallah, in writing her short stories, has used a blend of both the classical and the colloquial. In her narrative she has employed a poetic, evocative, classical language, rich in imagery and metaphor. The challenge to any translator is in the faithful interpretation of the poetry and imagery, and in retaining the atmosphere evoked and the cultural flavour. However, a greater challenge is in translating the colloquial language used by some of Emily Nasrallah's characters and maintaining the integrity of the meaning.

Another challenge is the portrayal of the Lebanese village in Emily Nasrallah's writing. Although many of the stories take place in the city, Beirut, one cannot escape the knowledge that Emily's roots are deeply entrenched in village life and culture, and her imagery is drawn almost exclusively from there.

The stories are being published under the subtitle *Stories from Beirut*. However, the events that take place are secondary to the *atmosphere* of war and destruction—the feelings of despair and hopelessness on the one hand and the fervent yearning for peace on the other.

It is my hope that these stories will be enjoyed by readers of English and will shed some light on the culture and region from which they emerge.

Thuraya Khalil-Khouri

CONTENTS

INTRODUCTION

When war broke out in 1975, Lebanon was basking in unprecedented social and intellectual affluence. There are those who would describe that era, from the mid-fifties to the mid-seventies, as the "Golden Age."

Two important factors that contributed to this development were the climate of liberalism, and the democracy that allowed for freedom of expression in writing and publishing. It is that climate which attracted to Lebanon, and to the capital, Beirut, in particular, the elite of Arab thinkers and intellectuals. In Beirut they found what they had been looking for: a city open to varied cultural experiences and able to assimilate the changes brought about by the twentieth century.

The women's movement, guided by a number of intellectuals, was not far removed from that atmosphere. The movement started mostly with middle class women who felt the need to acquire the responsibilities of leadership.

Women writers began to achieve a degree of confidence in themselves and their work that the pioneers before them had only dreamed of. They began to look towards a future in which their writing would become one of the pillars of an ancient and noble culture. The general atmosphere at that time was akin to the blossoming of flowers under the warm rays of a loving sun. Women were able to express themselves openly, presenting their most delicate and private feelings on the public stage of ideas with great faith and confidence. They felt they had now surpassed the journeys of the pioneers—those tentative and reluctant first steps—to stand by men in the march towards progress and creation. In fact, in many fields, women's ambitions drove them to compete with and surpass men.

However, just as there were those who supported and applauded, there were also those voices which rose in protest, denying women's courage and bravery. Women faced it all with honesty and dignity, leaving little room for doubts that might deter them from continuing their journey towards realizing their ambitions.

∞ Women's Literature

Lebanese women writers have dealt with a number of human and intellectual subjects. They have expressed themselves in poetry, short stories and novels, as well as in the fields of literary study and criticism. Since the Lebanese are fluent in more than one language, this multilingualism has been reflected in literary works written in Arabic, both classical and colloquial, and in French or English.

I, myself, have always rejected the idea of dividing literature into men's and women's, but I must admit that in most of what the Arab woman has written, the subject of her own self has remained most important: her own struggle for liberation and equality, her journey towards proving herself, her intellectual and creative achievements. She has written about her struggle against men, masters of her destiny; against her society and its belittling of her person and her efforts; and her struggle with herself, her worries, her fears, her ambitions, her victories and her losses.

In her dealings with everyday matters—social and human issues in general—she has remained different from her male counterpart because of the complexities involved in being an Arab woman.

∞ And then War ...

The war surprised her, as it had surprised all but a few in her country. It was a destructive, purposeless, chaotic war that burned in the streets of the cities and within the hearts of people. It was a war that exploded through her eyes and destroyed her dreams, levelled the cities she had written about in her stories—cities she had hoped would exist for her lifetime and the lifetime of her children.

She looked around with eyes that burned with the blaze of the fire, and she wondered: what had she done with her past? What would she do with her present? Would all that she had written and published and broadcast remain, would it have any value? Or had the past fallen away like the buildings that were being flattened around her? She had to start over again, rise from the ashes of the fires that burned everywhere.

∞ Ashes as the Source of Inspiration

The Arab woman writer left the past to history. From the shrapnel and the ashes she began culling her new material, to write of a new subject that had invaded her life, and imposed itself on her, on her loved ones and the future generations she was nurturing.

She found herself, in most instances, outside the battlefields. She was part of what, in Lebanon, was termed the "silent majority"—that is, the majority that receives the results of war, its destructions and tragedies. Women wrote from that position.

Since the Lebanese woman is far from the political scene and from the makers of political, economic, partisan and religious opinion, her literary work reflects that distance. It emphasizes the human aspects, the ability to hold on to the explosive moment, the feeling of living on the edge, the literature of martyrdom.

In *War's Other Voices*, a study on women and war, Miriam Cooke writes: "The men wrote from the epicentre. The men's writings catalogued savagery, anger and despair. The women's writings reflected the mood of the war and the emergence of a feminist consciousness."

I agree with that statement, and add to it that women also recorded the savagery of war, but used words as a means of self-defence and as a bridge to the future—nay, to salvation.

∞ War And Liberation

It is important to note a new experience for some young women in Lebanon during the war: they went into the streets and fought side-by-side with the men behind the barricades. That was during the two-year war, 1975-1976. It was an opportunity for these women to achieve an emancipation they had but dreamed about. "My one concern as I raided the streets to fight, was my right to be equal with the men, to take the decision in rejecting the traditional role of woman ... Behind the Doshka ... I found my freedom ..."

This quotation is taken from a study of young fighters entitled *The Klashnikov Generation* and conducted by Maroun Baghdadi and Nayla Dofreij after the two-year war. The voice of this woman is that of nearly every woman who went into battle to snatch for herself some form of freedom, at any risk, even death. The effects of this experience are reflected in the writings of a small number of writers closely related to the fighting either through religious, family or party loyalties. However, the predominant theme in mainstream women's literature was a humane outlook and a condemnation of war.

∞ Facing Reality

Women went through stages in what they wrote about war. At first there was shock at the horrors of war, as expressed by Hannan in my story *Those Memories* when she says, "It is incredible! Can you believe, Maha ... they brag about killing. One of them told me that he alone has killed one hundred and fifty people using a variety of methods. And when he'd had his fourth drink he began to describe to me the various hellish methods of torture and maiming—burning with electricity or cigarette butts; and amputations, especially amputating sexual organs. He said these were the most important part of the body and amputating them meant cutting out the roots. He's afraid his victims may grow roots that will come back to haunt him ..."

The next stage was meditating the past and the future before the anger exploded in revolt or total despair, as the other heroine in the above-mentioned story demonstrates: "The most I can hope for now is comfortable sleep. Sleep that is uninterrupted by the sound of explosions and shooting. I run away into sleep. I wish that entire day were night ..."

Should she sleep? Should she forget? Or should she stay and ponder, review and reassess her relationship with herself and all those who are dear to her?

The picture in front of her is unclear—especially the picture of the man. He is still the lover, the brother, the father, the son and the friend. But he is, at the same time, the force that pulls the trigger, explodes the bomb, launches the rocket and aims his sniper bullets at her chest. He is the hero and the malefactor at once, the noble one and the vile despicable one, the protector and the reason for despair. How is she to deal with this newly emerging picture of him?

Answering this question requires a study in human relations, particularly the relationship between men and women during the sixteen years of war. As for the women writers, the word has become a refuge and a life boat—the poem or story, a substitute nation.

Emigration, too, became another face of war, either for security, family or economic reasons. The emigration of the writer allowed her contact with new and diverse cultures. But it was also the most painful experience a writer or artist could go through: the uprooting, the loss of her connection to her culture and her land.

It is from this climate that I chose the stories published in this collection. They are a living testimony, rising from the core of fire and destruction. They are the stories of victims, not heroes. And in my opinion, a majority of the Lebanese were victims of a war that tore into the fabric of their being and their nation.

As a writer who has lived through the tragedies of her people and her country, and who sees similar tragedies unfolding with similar peoples around the world, I have to ask what effect this writing has. I must ask if the word still possesses the power to champion right—does it still possess the strength to carry the cries of the destitute and oppressed? And I must ask if there are still, in a world filled with the clamour of war machinery, ears that can hear the moans of the weak and the cries of the desperate.

Emily Nasrallah

Explosion

I do not know who records these words for me. Is it the pen that fled from me in the middle of the road as I ran, dragging my daughter behind me, to reach the nearest shelter? Or is it my body that was lifted from underneath the rubble and the ruins of the inferno to be stuffed into the plastic bag that would become its second skin?

When I speak of the "body," I am talking of what is left of it: the lumps and masses of flesh—skinned, flayed and torn—that bear no resemblance to the tall, svelte figure that had walked into the supermarket earlier, juggling the car keys in one hand and with the other clutching the hand of beautiful, little Neinar.

∞

Neinar, the pride and joy of her parents' hearts, the apple of their eye, flower of the four seasons, offering every day a new colour and a fresh fragrance. On that day, a Saturday as I recall, she woke early, came to my bed and shook me awake.

"Get up."

"What is it, my love?" I asked, as I rubbed remnants of sleep from my eyes.

"Get up ..." she repeated the order. "You promised me that today we'd go to the supermarket that sells the Cabbage Patch doll. I want a Cabbage Patch doll."

I smiled and hugged her, trying to entice her with the warmth of my embrace, but she would not be diverted. She would not climb into bed with me and snuggle in my lap and fill me with the essence of her being. She was adamant in her insistence on going to the supermarket, her single-minded purpose for the day.

I asked her, making light of the matter, "And did you dream of the Cabbage Patch doll in your sleep?"

She did not like my question and did not answer me, but kept pulling at my fingers.

∞

In truth, I had decided two days before to devote a couple of hours of my Saturday to buying the household necessities—things that a home consumes with an insatiable appetite. Neinar's little dream coincided well with my carefully laid out plans for that day. For I am a working mother and must plan every minute of my day to please the Lord and please the Boss and please the Family Head.

∞

"We have two hours and the supermarket is not too far. I just hope the highway is not as crowded as it normally is," I said to Neinar.

She did not seem to be listening to me. I looked at her in my rear view mirror. Eyes averted toward the window, she was contemplating the sea absentmindedly, recording all she saw in front of her, giving herself up to a childish wonderment and astonishment. She had forgotten I was there and was deaf to my babbling.

I, on the other hand, was very happy at having reconciled my duties and my daughter's outing. I decided I would take this opportunity to make it up to Neinar for the times I am at work, absent from her. The rest of our day would be filled with as many happy and pleasant moments as possible.

Parking the car not far from the store, I opened the back

door to help Neinar climb out. We walked towards the store. Or, rather, *I* walked; she ran and skipped and bounced about in circles like a bee. Neinar, my little bee with honey eyes and rosy lips and cheeks, and the fragrant flavour of a spring flower.

She went ahead to where the shopping carts were lined up, pulled one out and issued her orders.

"We start from here." Her little finger pointed to the toy section. I tried to convince her that we would return to that magical section after we had finished shopping for the necessities.

She was pleased with the arrangement, but looked up at me with a puzzled frown. "And the toys? Are they not necessary?"

I smiled to hide my unforgivable mistake. "They're the most important," I said. "That is why we're going to leave them until we're finished with all the bothersome things. That way we can devote all our attention to them."

She sensed the sincerity of my tone rather than understood the meaning of my words, and was placated. She walked next to me, occasionally stretching her arm toward the shelves to grab a box here or a bag there, to speed up the shopping process and get down to the *real* reason we had come to the supermarket.

∞

The store was crowded—not unusual for a Saturday. I saw a few friends accompanied, as I was, by children flitting around them awed and happy. They were out of their homes, and an outing these days, no matter how mundane, is more like a journey into the unknown ... but so are silence and noise, movement and action, alertness and lethargy. All of these words convey danger. For danger is no longer restricted to a time and place. It descends from the unknown, like a winged fate, spreading its feathers over the eves and rooftops of cities and suburbs. And when it folds its wings and flies away, it leaves behind ashes, remnants that barely hint that the place was once inhabited.

This is what happened a few days ago. It is all that remains within this memory as it strolls among the people and with them. Every movement, every turning, each activity brings back the reasons for our anxiety, nay, our terror. Even as we seek solace in forgetfulness, we find ourselves returning to burn in the hell of our memories. Yesterday, *Sad el Bawshrieh*, and before it *Sin el Fil*, and before that *Bir al Abed*; and before it and after it and as a result of it and following it ... Here and there and everywhere death stalks like a rabid monster, with no end in sight; and no sign as to where, when or how he will pack up and leave us.

∞

"It's a new doll, Mama. In Arabic it's called The Cabbage. It's like a cabbage all wrapped up in cloth. Nana bought one from London, and Joujou's aunt got her one. And you? Will you buy one for me? I love it, Mama. I love it more than anything."

Neinar took the doll without permission. She held it to her and turned round in a little dance, kissing it, hugging it ... inciting my jealousy.

When I was young we did not have this variety and abundance of toys. The most we had would be a dry stick, a button rejected from the sewing basket, a piece of cloth, a bit of cotton, residues of the sieve, threads. Then the creative process would begin.

A few hours later these sundries would become a rosy-cheeked, red-lipped doll, its hair tied back in a bun or falling coquettishly around its shoulders. Once that creative stage was completed we reached the naming stage. We would choose names that did not exist in the village roster: Marzipan, Furfur, Shenshen, Tuta. Names our imaginations were rife with, meaningless words that only became significant when given to our creations.

Neinar's generation is a lucky one. They receive their

dolls wrapped in lace. No effort required; no sewing or pasting; no anxiety that their creation would turn out to be a monstrosity eliciting snickers and mockery from the other children.

In fact, this Cabbage Patch doll, that so awed my daughter and others of her age, could be considered a missing link—something between a human form and a monster. Could this be why they are so attached to it? Or is it merely the result of creative marketing?

Why did I waste my time with such analysis? The important question was: would I pay the exorbitant amount for this awkward, clumsy-looking doll?

Of course, such thoughts I kept to myself. Who dares denigrate this queen of dolls, this Madame Cabbage! Who dares destroy a child's dream? I do not deny that I did try to dissuade Neinar from her choice. I pointed out to her all the other conventional dolls. Dolls, inspired by the great era of international cinema, wearing the faces of Ava Gardner, Grace Kelly, Greta Garbo, Marilyn Monroe.

But she turned away from them all, "Old fashioned faces ... not for our age!" she said.

I understand my daughter well. She knows her mind and what she wants. She possesses a keen sense and is able to go to the heart of matters. But I did not, apparently, know her that well. I did not imagine that she would be capable of categorizing in this manner, drawing sharp dividing lines between generations. I should have known that what pleases me shouldn't necessarily please her.

She finally put a stop to my interference and forced me to slip my hand into my purse to count the money I had left. Postponing this was out of the question. I could not bring her home disappointed. Not when she had been such a good girl. She looked at me, her gaze penetrating, touching the most vulnerable part of me, saying wordlessly, "It is now your turn. Will you keep *your* promise to me now?"

I opened my mouth to appease her, my hand still

roaming inside my purse, to tell her that the money I have on me is enou ...

I do not continue.

I open my mouth, and cannot close it again. I feel it tearing, ripping out of its place. I slip my hand in my purse, but my purse flies away from me—as does my shopping cart, stacked with my purchases; the people; the mothers with their carts, surrounded by flocks of angels; the store clerks; the piles of merchandise; the shelves; the cash registers; the surveillance equipment; the entrance door; the exit door. Nothing is left on which to rest the eyes. I feel my daughter is still near me. Neinar. Where has Neinar gone? She was holding the cabbage doll in her arms, clutching it to her chest, resting her cheek on its head. She was with me ...

With me?

Who is me? Who am I? I am no longer here. I am not there. Faster than the speed of lightning I become dis-jointed ... my parts scattered all around the place. But then there is no longer a place ... no longer a time.

I admit I did not hear the explosion. Maybe I lost my ears before the sound could reach me.

Maybe, I say, because there is no longer any certainty. I am scattered in the corners. My legs remain standing, like the barks of an oak. Then they take off, on their own, aimlessly.

The wings of my memory flutter and I see Neinar's face. No, not her face ... but an apparition, passing at a distance of years away ... Then I see it coming toward me and I nearly cry out with joy. But where will my cry come from? I have no throat, no vocal cords ...

∞

There is my purse.

My memory records it. I see it squeezing through the crowds, looking for a way out. Then it falls. Gone are my possessions—papers, money, identification. They all flee the purse to escape through one of the doors ... But there are no doors, they too have collapsed ... they are no longer doors. The ceiling is open to a sky that rains fire and metal.

Yes ... I remember the smoke in the hall. Thick smoke. Smoke softens the shapes and edges of things, but once it disperses, things return to their original lustre. This was a different kind of smoke, I knew that. The smoke was rising from the site of the explosion, expanding, mushrooming, spreading left and right, upward and downward, seeping into the pores. It was not the benign smoke of a country chimney or a campfire. It was a smoke that held within it the explosion of wrath and fury and the power of enmity.

∞

I hope now you will allow me to stop my narrative, after all that I have told you. My lips have parted company with each other, my joints are severed and scattered, part of me is burnt, charred.

And my little flower, my fragrant, sweet rose, Neinar, how is she to leave the store without her doll? And I remember ... I did not pay for it ... although there is still enough money left in my purse.

A House Not Her Own

The key is in her hand yet the door remains locked. The key does not find its way into the lock nor does the door respond. And for the tenth time she remembers: this is not the key to this door. It is the key that glues itself to her fingers every time she puts her hand in her purse. It is attracted to her by a magnetic power. She banishes it again to a separate pouch in her bag and looks for the other key.

The door opens and she hesitates for a moment before entering the apartment. She listens intently, for fear there may be someone inside. "Someone" who does not know her, who will pounce at her and ask her who she is. Her words would trip over each other.

She stands bewildered and confused. What would she tell her interrogator? Would she say why she is here? The questioning voice would come back to her from the inside and she would remain on the doorstep, silent. She would decide not to say anything, for there are no words to explain why she is here.

"*So, why* ... ?" She hears the voice of the beautiful woman, emanating from the picture in the gilded frame in the centre of the salon. It screams at her and she trembles, and shivers run from her head down to her toes.

"I thought you knew," she mutters.

The beautiful woman retreats and her voice loses its

harshness. *"They told me. They wrote to me from Beirut and they told me."*

"So they wrote ..."

"Yes, but I forgot ... I thought you were another."

"You are right. How are you to know me, we have never met." She hangs her head low.

∞

This is not the first time she enters this strange apartment. She has been here for more than a week. That is, since a rocket, of a calibre she does not remember, hit her house; her beautiful house in the middle of its glorious garden in the suburb of Beirut. The rocket took it upon itself to erase all traces of her house and eradicate her garden. She can but thank the Lord that she and her family managed to escape unscathed.

A thousand thanks to God.

They had been hiding in the basement of a neighbouring building. Small houses such as hers were not built for war. Nor were the bigger houses, she muses, thinking of the sights she had witnessed on her way from the ruins of her home to the city centre. Those sights convinced her that neither palaces nor skyscrapers nor fortresses were made to withstand the might of the modern artillery being experimented with in her country. Nothing could stand up to the concentrated shelling, the random shelling, the sporadic shelling. She witnessed the incredible and said to her sorrowed soul, "Your anguish is equal to that of others."

She repeats the adage to herself often. Not because she feels she is above other people or her despair is more important but because, at certain points in their lives, people forget that they are but ashes and dust. There are times when they believe they are omnipotent giants, their shadows extending as far as their eyes can see. And one day they receive a blow, they know not from where, and they awaken and they look around them and they are finally aware of their time and their place.

She has lost her home. She is now in this strange dwelling that was offered to her and her family by an old friend from college. "It is fully furnished," the friend told her. "The owners asked me to take care of it while they're away." Her friend gave her the key.

She is lucky. She has not ended up on the streets, nor out in the open, sleeping on the beaches like the thousands of destitute. She was lucky to have had a friend in her time of need.

∞

She takes another step towards the living room. Instinctively she places her package on the hall table. The package tilts, it is too big for the table. It topples the statue of a Greek god. She rushes back to the table, rights the *objet d'art*, gathers her purchases and retreats to the bedroom with them, muttering apologies.

Her guilt has been constant since she set foot in the strangers' apartment, since she first attempted to open the door with the wrong key. She walks through the apartment, apologizing to the tiles as she treads heavily on them. She places her possessions on a table. She hears the ghosts around her grumble. Children poke their heads out of the picture frames and shout at her, *"This is our place ... You belong elsewhere."* Their innocent smiles become ferocious, like shrapnel they cut into her flesh.

And the pretty woman in the big framed picture, holding up the cascading folds of the wedding dress she wore half a century ago, runs towards her, *"What hole did you creep out of?"*

Her groom shakes his head, tugs at his bow tie and speaks softly, *"She might have lost her way. Be gentle with her. Don't frighten her."*

Then they all shout from the walls, from behind the masks of time and dust. The voices of parents and grandparents, aunts and uncles, the living and the dead intermingle, *"Throw her out. She's a stranger. This house is not her own."*

"You are right. All of you are right. I am only here for a short while. My house was demolished by a rocket ..." But she does not continue for they have turned away and become deaf to her explanations.

She moves her things to the dressing table and is confronted by the army of bottles and jars lined up there and the souvenirs hanging on both wings of the mirror. She moves some of them to make room for her hairbrush and her few toiletries. "Excuse us," she murmurs. "We are only here for a short time." And she catches herself in her little dramatic moment and wants to laugh and cry at once. She collapses onto the nearest chair.

∞

In her dreams, during her childhood and youth, she imagined many scenarios, drew many images for her life, but never did she imagine her present situation. She never thought, not in her wildest dreams, that she would one day take refuge in a house not her own.

She always thought the house that would hold her, and the one she loved, would be hers forever. In childhood she had pictured it as a mud hut, on the banks of a stream among the orchards in her village. And as she grew so did her dream house. It grew taller as she grew taller. But even when it was only a tree house in her father's garden, or a tent atop their summer house, it remained special. Hers. The place where she could rest and dream, to which she could invite her friends. It remained open and welcoming.

Her words tumble and fall into the bottomless void. All that is left of her past now are words. Words and memories to be planted in the silence of this place and the emptiness of this time. She tells herself, "We are but passers-by on this earth. No sooner do we arrive than we are carried away by wings that lift us to a place where neither our plans nor our schemes matter. A place even our imagination is powerless to describe."

And a voice answers her, *"But people are like trees whose*

branches cannot grow the leaves of life unless their roots are firmly planted in the soil."

Ever since she had been pulled out by her roots and implanted in this new soil she has felt dizzy and numb. She holds her head in her hands, lest it, too, should fall off. Her head reels with the voice and its echo. She has to learn how to cope with the new reality.

∞

A quarter of a century written with blood and tears, in which she built her home like a female bird builds her nest. She and he, both, against the fates. A blessed life it had been. The seeds of blessing having been planted beneath the foundations of her home, for stone and steel and wood do not make a home. Nor does luxurious furniture dictated by the fancy and whim of decorators and creative strangers. What good is it for a house to withstand the elements if the gentle breeze of love and life does not blow within? What is the meaning of a home if it is a cocoon closed to the world, and the world's dreams and magic? What is the meaning of her existence in this strange place where the walls are but stone and the doors planks of wood? And what if it were an expensive ebony? It is still only wood, and the marble is icy beneath her feet and the ceiling threatens to cave in on her.

She rises from her seat and moves aimlessly through the rooms and onto the balcony. There is the sea, a blue expanse, cold and remote. It reminds her of the Arctic ocean that she had once visited. And the buildings, shoulder to shoulder, hugging, each trying to hide the other's faults, the roads winding around them, grey and paved in dust. She can hear the children's cries coming at her from every direction. They hang in the air, strangely devoid of childish joy. In front of her are the balconies of neighbouring buildings, decorated with clotheslines— the trademarks of the dispossessed. She remembers that she is but a drop in this vast ocean of misery, a grain of sand on its shores. Yet she gives herself and her feelings so much importance. She wraps herself in her cloak of misery and turns this apartment into a cocoon that threatens to suffocate her. What is wrong with her? She, who even in her first home, the little village on the slopes of Mount Haramoun, had an unquenchable thirst to better herself, to learn, to rise in the world, to delve into the mysteries of the universe.

∞

Her feet lead her around the apartment. Questions rise from deep within her, turn in an empty circle, and remain in search of answers. From which direction will her answers come?

From the West? Where the warships are anchored, spewing fire and destruction onto the land? From the North where the north winds blow icy cold, cutting into the flesh like the blade of a knife? Or from the East where the battles rage and the fronts are aflame; where explosives roar like thunder and ululating bullets write, in red and yellow fire upon the night sky, the names of those that have fallen? Or is it from the South that she will get her answers? The South!

She wraps her arms around herself as though hiding from the danger around her. Her body has become weak as a child's, left unprotected, at the mercy of the elements. She holds her body with her arms, trying to build fences around it. Then she realizes that her arms are powerless to protect her battered body, for they are part of it. And the protection she so dearly desires at this moment will not come from any earthly source.

∞

She is awakened from her deep thoughts by a fierce banging on the door. She turns around and automatically walks towards the door, not asking who it is. She reaches out to open it, then retreats. She remembers where she is. She remains in her place, fixed, listening to the banging grow louder and fiercer, beating at her like a hammer.

Slowly, she withdraws to the farthest corner of the house, for she is not expecting anyone ... and the house is not her own.

How We Were

I held onto your hand and your soft, delicate fingers intertwined with my big, coarse ones that were offspring of the oak and the sumac trees. And through the pores invisible sap communicated to you my warmth. Happiness blossomed in your innocent eyes as you skipped along the sidewalk near the blue sea. Your free hand gestured toward the horizon and your stammering lips said, "Sea gull …"

As though the gull heard the echo of your words and thought them a summons, it approached the shore where we stood. Your eyes were fixed upon the path it traced in the sky. When it was only metres from us, it dove into the water and retrieved a small fish. Dumb and cocky, the fish had been attracted to the surface of the water by the dancing lights. After regaining its balance, the gull flapped its wings and flew away. We continued on our way, on our slow, peaceful walk.

On one tranquil morning we saw a number of other people ambling along, too. Young and old, mothers and children. They were strolling down the sidewalk which opened like a lover's arms, welcoming their happy faces, carrying them atop its solid, cobbled surface, that they might enjoy the mixed blueness of the sea and sky.

On those mornings, and on mornings following them, and the ones after those, we went out to walk by the sea, and were met by faces that grew familiar. We exchanged greetings without words. We shared the silent understanding of our common goal.

You began to grow. Your soft, delicate fingers separated from my big, coarse ones. I stood aside and observed you as you skipped sometimes like a bird, or hopped like a rabbit in the stillness of the wild. The threads of time stretched out, carrying with them the multicoloured bubbles of our happy times together.

Sometimes, when you met children of your own age, you slowed down. You watched them, smiled at them and spoke to them. And soon enough it happened—you entered their world and forgot me, some distance behind you, just a person who watched out for you. And when you remembered me again and came back, you found my arms trembling with the yearning to hold you.

Sometimes we were content to sit on one of the stone benches; your legs swinging in a failed attempt to reach the ground.

We passed the time tattling—questions from you and answers from me. At times we reversed roles: I asked and you answered. Your words transported me into the wondrous, marvel-filled world where children reside on crystal islands populated with vast forests of imagination.

Many a time I attempted to penetrate that world but was unable to even cross the threshold, let alone enter it. Adults were barred from the magical world that opened only to the flutter of young wings.

I remember during one of our talks asking you, "If I became a child again, would you allow me into your world?"

You looked up at me, your eyes filled with wonder and confusion and a great deal of misgiving. "If ..." you said. Then, as though saving yourself from falling into error, continued, "But grown ups cannot become children."

"If children can grow into adults, why can't adults

return to their original state ... they used to be children before?"

Without missing a beat, you answered, "Because they are out of the game."

At times the sun deserted the beach, leaving a grey cloud cover that stretched out of the blueness of the sea and upwards as far as the eye can see. We walked through the fog and eavesdropped on the waves as they whispered to those who caressed their cheeks and kissed their mouths in play. And when the whispers turned to howls and roars we ran and hid behind the glass windows and watched how the threats and warnings were to be executed.

In that long ago time, you were my little girl, and I was your mother. Then your little footsteps bolted away from the runway within my heart, and you soared.

I had no idea that between the flutter of an eyelid and the ticking of seconds you were learning how the seagulls soar. I did not know that you were filching the secret of mastery over me, while I watched your shadow jumping, from between my eyelids, surrendering stupidly to my ecstasy.

And during one of those moments of surrender and deceptive peacefulness, you withdrew, your little footfalls becoming giant footsteps.

The little fingers, that had received the sap of my love and the warmth of my being, expanded ... Expanded and extricated themselves from mine. They were transformed into the strong wings of a seagull, and you soared into space ... into the limitless universe.

I returned from my wearisome voyage to rest on the old stone bench, on the sidewalk by the sea, after the exhaustion of attempting to catch up with you. I looked for the seagulls in vain, I searched for the light in vain.

Grey clouds enveloped the buildings and descended to wrap the blueness of the sea, and silence the chuckle of waves.

I said to myself, "It is autumn. Why am I trying to penetrate this clear, calm surface? This natural autumn scene? It is an autumn cloud caressing the surface of the water, and it will soon clear. And the water will be blue and clear, and will tremble with the stroking of the breeze."

And I said, "This is but a temporary state and it will soon dissipate and happiness will once more return to dance within my heart and my eyes, as I watch over you running and skipping … as I run after you with all the strength and energy I can muster, my voice reaching you ahead of me, to support you should you fall."

I told my soul, comforting it, lifting it out of its wearying anxiety, "We will be back. We will return to how we were in the past. And you will be my little one again. Your velvety fingers will hold on to my thick rural ones. We will run together by the sea, facing the mountain, over the cobbled sidewalk."

But the doubts that rise from that truth are like a dagger in my throat. Soon they become a scream that demolishes the dream and shakes the foundations of illusion.

I see you suddenly as you truly are. A young woman, pure as the light of day. You are not a seagull, you are no longer a child who skips along as I chase after her.

Our childhood talks hung still on the invisible threads of time. I saw them sometimes moving, shivering like the autumn leaves.

I tried to grasp at some of them with my hands, those childhood conversations, to put them in an envelope and send them to you.

I told myself, "Tread softly on the sidewalk by the sea and listen carefully, for the waves may have retained some of what has slipped through the cracks of memory. You may find a picture stolen by the seagulls and hidden in their secret caves among the rocks." I said all that to myself to silence the anxiety storming through me, quaking within me, and to fill the bottomless void inside me.

My grown little one, you continued your journey, you have not stopped. You skipped over the sidewalk by the sea, and rode on the wing of a seagull (or an airplane, to me they are no different ... they have taken you away from me, snatched you away when your down was not yet sturdy enough).

You did not choose your distance, nor did I. It was imposed upon us by another, stronger will.

And when I saw you ambling among the fields of that faraway continent, replacing the sidewalk by our warm sea with that distant shore so close to the North pole, I wept.

I have wept a great deal since we were separated. Not for myself ... but because the separation was the one event that I had not been expecting, that I had not prepared for ... and because the mother bird does not push its chicks off the bough, out of the nest's warmth, to learn how to fly, until she is certain that their down is complete and their wings fully mature, able to carry them away safely to their destinies.

That was not what happened with us. That is why I came back, to walk over the sidewalk of our past, thinking of you, dreaming of you, talking to you. Saying, "I may have you again some day." When the simmering fates let up, and the volcanoes calm down. I will get you back again with blooming flowers and baskets-full of the fruit you picked along your journey into different worlds that have opened up to you, welcomed you, invited you within to explore their essence and their meaning. But what I do not know is how you will return.

When ... ? When will it come about?

As I await the answer, my little one who has so suddenly grown, I continue to walk along the sidewalk by the sea during the light of day and the dark of night. I am here on the sidewalk you have known, now that night's mysterious armies have landed. The amblers have deserted their shore, the sun forsaken the horizon, and with it the bevy of gulls. Nothing moves save the slight trembling of the tree tops, and the soft twitching of the water, like the sound of one who is enjoying the rehashing of memories.

As I make ready to leave with those who are leaving, I see you coming towards me. Suddenly you are here, the way you were with me during our past walks. I stretch my arm out to hold your hand and your soft fingers intertwine with the coarseness of mine. You spring along with happy steps, chasing a bird that tries to rejoin the flock, after being caught unawares by the night.

We discover together that the night will not hinder its attempt to join its friends. And with the sound of its flapping wings, I hear the echo of a phrase that has become my mantra, the prayer I offer to the world: How we were in the past ... when you were my little girl.

The Nightmare

I remember only the wide expanse of the place, the spiral and straight staircases surrounding it. I was with a group of friends. It is difficult now to remember their names, but they were friends. In smile and glance and gesture and company, they were my friends.

I felt warm and content. Nothing disturbed me. I was not hot nor cold nor hungry nor full. There was nothing to complain about. I flung myself down and floated on an ocean of contentment, no care or burden weighing me down.

I was in ecstasy, experiencing that nirvana-like state one captures fleetingly only in dreams. And all that's left, upon awakening, is the memory of it as it seeps slowly through the pores and is lost. Any attempt to grasp it, to hold on to it, will end in failure, for dreams devour dreams as we are expelled into the dawn of a new day. Awake, and only half alert, we go about our lives, seeking our livelihood, a place in the sun, a shelter for our heads, an ear to listen to us, an eye to watch over us, a hand to guide us, a heart to take pity on us.

From the very depths of my dream I return. Like a refreshing, invigorating flood of cool water washing over an over-heated body, rapture engulfs me.

I rise from the depths of the dream into ... a nightmare.

I was in a large chamber so wide and spacious I could

see no end to it. There was no furniture, only staircases everywhere, all around. Some going up, higher and higher into nowhere, some going down to the depths of the earth. I was surrounded by a group of friends, happiness and warmth shining from their faces.

One of them suggested we have lunch at his home. It was noontime, there was nothing pressing to do. We all agreed. We walked to his house, a tightly knit group. We drew closer to each other until we became as one. Regardless of the different heights, weights, shapes, we made one huge human mass. And we rolled on, like a giant ball, towards our friend's home.

Two men appeared. Two strangers.

They came towards us with strong, confident steps. Upon reaching us, one of them grabbed the arm of a man in our group and pulled him away from us. He did not have to exert much effort to do so, for the man surrendered peacefully and docilely to them.

"My father ... That's my father!" I said to the person closest to me. "Where are they taking him?"

My words reached my father and he turned to me, his look serene and peaceful, and he murmured, "Do not fear, my dear. I am going on a small mission."

"That's right," said one of the two men, "a mission."

Then he turned around and said to me, "He's going with us on a mission. We need his expertise."

With those words he put his arm around my father's broad shoulders while the other did the same from the other side. And my father became their hostage—at their mercy and at the mercy of their whims.

I could do nothing. I could not act. I was limited by the time and the place I was in. The walls of my fate surrounded me and I was able to do nothing. There was no trace of my friends, the people who had been invited to lunch. I was alone in that wide expanse of endless space.

There was nothing I could do but weep. And so I wept, my tears rising from the very depths of my soul, fearful and savage. I cried the tears of the bereft and the grieving, those who had lost a loved one, and with him all hope and life.

I am not sure how long I wept, but I am sure that it was not too long before I found myself drowning in my tears. The tears flowed from my eyes and made rushing rivers that joined a sea of tears whose waves engulfed me, bathed me, swallowed me and nearly drowned me. And all I could do was shed more tears. I was crying for the man who had been taken away by the two thugs, his expression complacent, his words comforting, saying he was in the company of friends and there was nothing for me to fear, his eyes telling me of his love and affection for me.

I was weeping for my helplessness and powerlessness and the helplessness of all those around me, none of whom could lift a finger in his aid. I was crying for the group of people who had appeared to me as whole and solid in their unity, who moved as one and in one direction, but who did nothing for the man who was snatched away from their midst. I was crying for myself, for having done nothing, like them.

Why had I not shouted at the men, told them I knew they were not friends? I knew what they were doing. Such behaviour is not unfamiliar to me. I had seen it before. Is that not the savage, merciless treatment of wild animals towards their prey since prehistoric times, since people were cave dwellers? No. Wild animals are honourable and dignified and courageous. They face their prey and do not trick them. They allow them to defend themselves if they can.

In my anguish and my shame I admitted I was a coward. And the friends who were with me were cowards. They lifted not a finger to help him. They disappeared, vanished into the air like a puff of smoke. And they left me all alone with my helplessness, my legs too weak to carry the burden of my guilt.

I wanted to follow the two men. Just to make sure. Maybe I *had* misjudged them. Maybe they really did need my father's expertise. Maybe it was not a trick, not a lie. But how was I to move out of this sea of tears that had engulfed me and that grew deeper and higher as I shed more tears?

∞

Finally, I stop crying; or my tears run dry. I open my eyes, and all of a sudden, I see ... nothing. Nothing save the darkness that envelops my room and my soul. And slowly a shaft of light filtering through a crack grows wider and bigger.

"It's dawn ..." I say to myself. "It's dawn—that means my salvation is near."

I reach out my hand to feel the water around me and am surprised to find it has receded, leaving me lying on my bed. "It is just the confusion of my dreams," I say to myself slowly, hesitantly, as though waiting for a response.

It's a nightmare, says a voice from within me. *A nightmare made of salt and water and darkness ...*

"Thank goodness I have come out of it whole!"

I am safe and whole. I have not lost any part of my body, or any of my senses. But my father ... where is my father? ... Where did I leave him and what has happened to him? Is he still being held prisoner by the two strangers? And have they taken him hostage in exchange for one taken from them?

The questions come down on me like the beating of a hail storm. I throw off the covers, jump out of bed, rush to my window. I push aside the curtains in an attempt to untie the knots of darkness that hold me. The sun is bright, not a sign of the storms of the night before. The sky is clear, the sea calm after the tempest. White birds hover just above the water's surface and the street welcomes the day's activities.

"Ah, a beautiful day. Like the first day of creation." I say the words out loud, involuntarily.

A voice from my depths answers, *What has nature to do with your condition? This is another attempt at escape on your part.*

"No, it is a rescue attempt. Escapism was the dream. I am now awake. This is reality."

In wakefulness there is an escape of a different kind. Wakefulness shrouds your consciousness in life's daily burdens, and the darkness of reality dissipates with the coming of daylight ...

"Is this reality?" I wonder as I open the door to meet the people congregated on the streets of life and action.

And then I see them. Each one of them. The friends who had accompanied me in my dream, the ones who had disappeared and left me in the wasteland, abandoned and alone.

I do not go near them this time, for my wounds are still open and festering, and they hurt. I turn away from them to the direction in which the two strangers had taken my father. But I can see no sign of them, nothing that tells me how or where my kidnapped father is.

An ice-cold wind gusts from the tops of the mountains where eagles build their nests. It seeps through my pores and gets into my head and dispels the cobwebs left by years of dreams and realities, and I remember. I remember that my father could not have been there when the two strangers arrived into my dream.

It is impossible for him to have been there. The man who is responsible for my existence, whose arms cradled me, who gave me life and brought me from nonexistence to birth, no longer belongs to this world. One autumn evening years ago, like a bird that flaps its wings and flies away to warmer, more pleasant climes, he flapped the wings of his soul and flew away. I was not there to witness the ecstasy of his liberation from earthly bonds. I was not there to see him shake off the earth's dust from his body.

I was not with him when the two thugs sneaked into his home and tricked him and took him away.

And he, for the purity of his conscience, for the kindness of his heart, for his trust and faith in men, for his innocence and love and for many other reasons that are unknown and cannot be told, went with them. He thought the hand extended to him a friendly one, not knowing that behind it were the hands of a thousand executioners.

It is the nightmare that sits so heavily upon my chest with the coming of darkness, crushes my ribs, pierces my eyes until I cry rivers.

It is a nightmare. Reality, rising from behind the rubble and the debris, confirms this. My happiness, at awakening, at being saved, is not in vain.

My father is dead. One autumn evening he flapped his wings and, like an eagle tired of living on the low ground, he soared into the sky, following the line drawn by the hand of fate.

I thank God that my father died before *these* thugs could take him away.

Once again.

Yearning

There was a light tapping on my door. I thought I was dreaming. I was alone at home and it was after midnight, so I thought I must be dreaming. I made no effort to open my eyes or get out of bed to open the door. But the tapping recurred, soft and rhythmic.

I jumped out of bed and stood behind my closed door whispering, "Who's there? Who is it?" But I received no answer. My heartbeat quickened: who visits at this time of the night? Who would knock on my door at this hour and fill me with dread? Who would even dare open their door on this battle-heated Beirut night?

My questions stopped when I realized that this was my bedroom door and not the main entrance to the house—the entrance that one would normally use to get indoors.

My heart went into a panic. Someone could be inside the house. Someone could already have invaded my home, using the force of weapons, as is often the case in these broken times.

But no, I must be imagining things. My imagination running wild again. Or maybe I just forgot to lock the front door.

Yes, that's probably exactly what happened. For I have begun to notice lately little holes gaping through the pages of my memory, and forgetfulness has become an inescapable reality for me. Haven't names started slipping away whenever the faces they belong to appear?

Can I deny that one morning I even forgot my own name and spent a few seconds drowning in embarrassed silence? Is it any wonder, in the light of all that has happened and has taken place, and all that is happening and is yet expected to happen, that I would forget to close my front door?

But I thought again. And my thoughts cancelled out all my doubts, assuring me that this could not have been the case. I could not have left the front door open. Locking one's doors is no longer a habitual, reflex action you perform without a thought. In these days of war and destruction, locking doors has become a ritual that demands thought and time and planning. And I, like any citizen governed by the laws of the jungle, perform the locking-up operation with precision and efficiency, motivated by my survival instincts and the drive to cling to life.

To retire peacefully, I need to perform the ritual that would allow me that peace. I close the corrugated iron door, pulling at it with all my might, until it locks at the threshold, then I close the heavy wooden door. Then I pull the chain into its latch and I clamp a padlock over it. But I do not snap the lock until I have made sure the key to the main bolt has closed all the way, and I pull at it until my teeth grind together. Finally, I snap on the padlock, after making certain all the little openings and joints are closed to the outside world. Then—only then—do I move quietly to my bedroom. There I close the bedroom door—from the inside, of course, and do not feel safe until I have closed the shutters and the glass windows and drawn the thick curtains over them. But I never forget to leave the window panes slightly ajar lest they shatter with the force of the tremors reserved, usually, for volcanoes and other natural disasters. In our case, they are brought on by flying rockets and bombs that infiltrate our little alley.

Once I am sure that all security measures have been

taken, I can finally relax. Only then do I allow my weary body and wilting soul to surrender to sleep.

"He surrendered to a peaceful sleep," is an expression that creeps up from childhood memories and old essay books. We borrow it today to describe different situations, daily occurrences.

You can be sleeping soundly, sunk in a sea of dreams, when you are surprised by the sound of a bomb, or the explosion of a booby-trapped car beneath the window, or the ululations of a machine gun, or the screaming of anti-aircraft artillery, and rockets that explode inside your brain first and then spread to other parts of your body, until all your senses have sucked it in and it resides in the very depths of your subconscious.

Or maybe you are surrendering to the ecstasy of dreams that have become the only escape in our times—a place to run away to from the daily images of war that stab at you like sharpened spears.

Or you can be lulled into a false security, lifting your soul above the clouds where you can float in peace, until someone knocks at your door and disturbs your peace, drives you out of the dream, out of the ecstasy you seek, out of the fake security and false warmth.

Someone comes along and robs you of the freedom you attained through your own special means, and you may never be able to repeat it. Someone kidnaps you out of the remembered past, when you lived a normal life, when freedom meant the freedom to leave your home, to walk the streets, to swim in the sea, to visit the mountains—times when it did not take courage to fulfil your child's dream of taking him out for a drive, or a walk in the woods.

How did we not know that we would arrive at times like these? How did we not foresee that we would become as cowardly as alley rats? How did we not know that the rats would discard their skins and become the rulers of the streets?

Someone was still tapping gently on my door, while I stood behind the door and asked softly, "Who's there? Who knocks?"

The tapping continued and no one answered my question.

I had waited so long in vain. The tapping had not grown stronger nor had I gleaned any information from my repeated question. I was becoming more frightened and anxious. My doubts were growing. Was this reality or was it a dream?

Why couldn't it all be a dream? An illusion? Was I now rising from the depths of sleep? Our way of life has turned our nightmares into reality. And the two states have merged together with the frequency of bomb-interrupted sleep and heavy shelling. We no longer know dreams from reality; we no longer differentiate between the circle of peaceful, restful sleep and the maze of nightmares.

At that point I realized my thoughts had come full circle and I no longer had any choice but to surrender totally.

But surrender to whom, to what? To sleep again? Or to confrontation and wakefulness and bravery? How could I travel outside this circle that had transformed me in time and place and thrown me into a loop? How could I explain my feelings and sensations?

The gentle tapping returned. I grew silent. I tried with my silence to start a discourse with the unknown standing behind my door, maybe through telepathy.

I was not given more time for reflection, for the stranger entered my room suddenly, although my door remained firmly closed.

How could he have come in? I did not dare lift my gaze to him, and, of course, I did not have the courage to ask how he had managed to get in.

"Have you forgotten?" asked a gentle, pure voice that awakened within me dormant feelings and burst the dams that contained my tears.

"Have you forgotten?"

I knew this voice. I could feel it crawl over my skin, through my pores, throughout the rest of me.

"I know this voice!" I said out loud.

"Of course you know the voice," he said immediately. "Lift your eyes to me. Look at me."

"Father?" I screamed.

"Yes," he said calmly.

"But you are ..."

"Say it ... Don't be frightened of the word. Say it."

"But you have been gone for ..."

"Six years. And now I feel I want to pay you a visit. To check on you, that's all."

"But ... how?"

"You mean how did I get in? That was easy. Do you want the details?"

"No, no ... It is enough that you are here. The sweetness of love and warmth envelopes me. But tell me ..."

"Why did I come alone?"

"You're reading my thoughts. I never knew you could do that."

"It is a natural thing to do, in my new home. Where I have come from there are no longer any barriers. People are free beings who intermingle and interlace, and then separate like atoms in the air, without effort or sadness or anger."

"And Mother? I mean, are you ... together?"

"Yes. And we are as close as we always were. I cannot say we are husband and wife. In our new world those words have no place, no one understands them. But that does not prevent two beings from meeting and staying together for eternity, forming a union."

"Why didn't you bring her with you? My heart is breaking."

"Please, use simple words that I can understand."

"I long to see her."

"She visits you all the time."

"Yes, I know. But not the way you are visiting me now. She comes to me in dreams. You have opened a new door for communication."

"Don't talk like a fool. This door has been open since eternity, and it will be open forever."

"Now you are using complicated language, Father."

"Tit for tat."

"You have not lost your sense of humour. I always knew you would never change."

"Oh, but I have changed a great deal. Only you are unable to see it, for the old picture still blurs your vision."

"But this is your present picture. The way I see you now."

"It is a picture I borrowed from the past, so you would know me."

He said those final words and turned to face the door. I reached out to him swiftly with my hand. I did not know what I meant to do. Stop him from leaving? Keep him with me? Or touch the hand that had made no move to touch me?

Maybe I would say what I used to say as a child, "Take me with you ... I miss so much going for a walk with you."

I was confused, of that I was certain. My arm stretched out in the air and he faced the door, his back to me fading slowly, like a puff of smoke fades in the wind. He was gone and I had not had the chance to ask him: Do you feel as I do now? Does the yearning boil within your souls nearly melting them, as it does with us?

I did not ask my question. But I heard the whispered answer from behind the closed door, "Of course we yearn. Why else would we endure the journey to return?"

Andromeda:

The Golden Legend

I saw her standing on the edge, between the sand and the breaking waves. Her back was to the city, her eyes fixed on a distant point on the horizon. I was out on the beach for my daily walk before sunrise, before other humans awakened, before life stirred through the city's veins, before the sun filtered through the verdant city balcony that was my only link to nature.

It was natural that after seeing her I would continue on my way and forget about her. The beach is open to all creatures. So are those precious pre-dawn moments from which we snatch some faith and courage to go on.

She did not feel my presence or lend it any importance; she was absorbed in her musings, looking out, so I thought, toward the unseen. But I was wrong. As soon as I reached a point parallel to where she stood, she turned around and smiled at me.

She was a stranger to our city; a stranger to our land. Her flowing blue gown fell in folds to her feet. It was no ordinary gown—it was woven with threads taken from the sea and the sky, the wind and the clouds, and the sea foam. Her hair, high atop her head, was not real hair. It was a mixture of ropes of light and verdant greens and liquid gold. Her face imparted the notion of beauty, but it was a distant beauty, as though reflected through a mirror.

Her smile alone was able to pass through the barriers and reach me. It encouraged me to smile back and then move on. A feeling of dread came suddenly over me and I started to doubt my own senses.

But she did not allow me the chance to escape. From her parted lips came a cry, like that of a child, of such magnetic force it pulled me back to her until I was standing in front of her, unmoving, waiting, and ready to obey.

"I did not know you frequented this place," was the first thing she said to me.

I was surprised at that and told her so. Then I added, "Those are my sentiments exactly, for I take this walk along this beach every morning. I have never seen you here before."

She extend her slim, snowy white arm to me and put her hand on my shoulder. "You are right," she said. "I am very happy to have met you."

Her kindness encouraged me to carry on. "Do you come to this beach every morning?" I asked.

"Every morning at sunrise."

"You come here to walk?"

"To wait!" She was silent. She turned away from me and continued to watch the distant horizon.

I thought she had put an end to our conversation and I decided to walk away. But she turned around as though she had read my thoughts. She took my hand and said, "I am very glad you came."

"But I ..."

"I know ..." she interrupted without looking at me or telling me what it was that she knew. Then she continued, "I realize you need to walk. But it restricts you and you are seeking freedom."

"Yes, I know what you mean," I said indifferently, not interested in more details and explanations.

But she would not let me go. She went on to explain

how a habit can become a restriction, how one is never totally free until one is free of all habitual behaviour.

"But my daily walks are a way to freedom ..."

She interrupted me, "You mean a way towards movement. No, there is a difference between the two."

I did not answer. Not because I did not understand what she was saying, but because I had no intention of indulging in a discussion that would rob me of the opportunity to watch the sunrise and the changing colours of the world. Besides, opening up to strangers and delving into personal discussions with them was not an easy thing for me.

And who could this woman be? Why had she stopped me in the middle of my walk? Why was she tying me up in conversation, forcing me to think when I had come here to escape thought? And how should I talk to someone I did not know? Was she of our earth, or a figment of some imagination?

Before my anger could take over, she released my hand and set me free. But I found myself unable to depart, for I had not yet discovered who she was. I gathered my courage and asked, "Who are you?"

"Andromeda."

"Meaning?"

"The saviour of the city."

"This city, you mean?"

"This and others."

"Then tell me, Andromeda, when did you save our city, and how? It has been burning with the wars of the nations for more than ten years. Its children, young and old, are fodder for the fires that have devoured it, along with our mountains and valleys, yet the fires still rise up, immune to all attempts to contain them, as though they could go on for centuries. Tell me, for God's sake, when and how are you going to save our city?"

"I did save it. One thousand five hundred years ago."

"From the war?"

"From all catastrophes."

"This city in particular?"

"This one and others."

At this point I was silent, trying to make sense of the words. What did she mean by "save"? Was it a symbolic word with a meaning that I had failed to grasp? I asked her again, "How were you able to save all those cities?"

"By self-sacrifice," she answered immediately.

"*Your*self?"

"Can one *self*-sacrifice another?"

"But you are here now and you are alive, and this is a reality ..."

"That is what I intended you to understand."

But that, of course, was what I could not understand. I stood in front of her, confused and confounded. Words slid off her tongue easily, transparent and clear. Yet as soon as they were captured by the ears they became mysterious. I had thought words would be a way to unravel her identity. Now I found myself puzzled; afraid and puzzled.

I should leave at this point, I thought. Our meeting will remain just a passing adventure and this conversation will be forgotten. Getting involved any further could be unpleasant. Besides, what is the use of attempting to uncover her identity, when all her answers are symbols?

She drew me out of my silent contemplation and attempted to untie the knot—first, the knot that held up her hair. Her hair tumbled down her shoulders and cascaded to the surface of the sand. I was standing in front of an image from a fairy tale. Why is she doing this? I thought. Why did she release her hair? And is it really hair, or a tent made of gold brocade and sun rays? From within that tent, a voice, pure as a babbling brook, spoke: "The first time was a thousand five hundred years ago. My name was Andromeda, Princess, daughter of the king of the corals—his only child.

"My father's palace was the most beautiful in the

world. His reign the most just, his people the happiest and most secure. There were no conflicts. Each person knew his responsibilities and performed his duties loyally and honestly, and each knew his rights and was sure of their preservation with justice and righteousness.

"Then came a day that disturbed the joy of life and turned happiness into hardship. There rose from the depths of the sea a dragon. He began to plunder and pillage the city, destroy and ravage what the people had built, slaughter young men and women. We had no way of destroying him, for he was endowed with special powers that rendered him invisible. He would attack a place and ransack it, while remaining unseen.

"My father, his council and the city elders were confounded by the dragon. The kingdom could endure no more of this. Its people had become poor after having been wealthy, degraded after having been proud. The kingdom's treasurer presented my father with a report on the general condition of the kingdom; it would soon collapse if the dragon was not destroyed and his assault not stopped.

"My father was unable to confront the dragon on the field of battle. Our weapons failed against a creature that breathed fire onto a land and set it ablaze.

"Among my father's councillors was an old wise man who made a suggestion that was acceptable to the majority. He suggested that my father send a delegation of his most prominent citizens to negotiate a settlement with the enemy that would satisfy both parties.

"But they returned with a bigger problem. The monster, from his position of strength, had laid conditions. He would, he said, spare the people and their possessions, if the king would give him, every year, the most beautiful girl in the kingdom. Because there was no better solution, they accepted his condition.

"The king was a fair and wise man. He considered

every girl in the kingdom his daughter. It was natural that he would choose me to be the first sacrifice.

"My mother dressed me in finery; she put a priceless pendant around my neck, rings on my fingers, earrings for my ears, anklets around my ankles, and bade me farewell with a tear and a kiss.

"I had to walk a distance with the king and his council, until we reached a narrow path that led to the beach, where I would continue alone to the place where the dragon awaited me. That was what I did. I sat waiting for him with a sense of peace and resignation. I was surprised at the feeling of ecstasy that had overcome me instead of the fear and anxiety I had expected. Even after I saw him rise through waves, the water around him swelling to mountains, his mouth spitting fire and smoke, I felt no fear. When he appeared in front of me—only I could see him—I was not frightened. I did not leave my spot either. If he wanted me, he would have to come to me.

"He opened his enormous fiery mouth and released a peculiar vaporous substance that drew me toward him, and I felt, during those moments, that I would indeed become fodder for his fire ... But ... Good Lord! How did this staff appear in my hands? I asked myself, unbelieving. It was a long pole and it grew as I clutched it, turning this way and that of its own volition. As soon as I pointed it at the dragon, as a mysterious force ordered me to, he bent to his knees submissively, and began to retreat into the waves. It all happened very quickly and I remained there in shock, the staff in my hand, not comprehending what it was. But it was a great force which had helped me vanquish the dragon.

"This happened one thousand five hundred years ago, when a king withheld nothing from his people, even his most precious possession. When a princess did not forsake duty from fear, and went to the very extremes of giving and sacrifice. She would offer herself for her people and her kingdom's salvation and deliverance from slavery and degradation."

"And what happened after that?" I heard myself ask.

"From the day I left my father's palace I have not returned. I have been travelling among the vanquished cities of the world seeking out the dragon at the entrance to every city, to challenge him and fulfil my sacrifice. But my trusted staff comes to my rescue every time. And each time, I plunge it between the dragon's eyes and watch him retreat roaring, spewing flames and throwing himself into the waves until he disappears."

"Is that what you were waiting for this morning? For the dragon to appear upon the horizon?"

"You did notice, then? I have been waiting for him to appear for ten years. I come to the beach every day as I have done in other cities. I am ready for him, ready to execute the ultimate sacrifice. But why has he not appeared? That is what I want to know. He has never forgone a confrontation yet."

"What makes you so sure he will appear? What if he has changed his pattern? What if he has gone never to return?"

She gave me a scolding look and said, "He will come, just as he did one thousand five hundred years ago. Have you not felt his hot breath in the city streets? Tell me, have you not seen signs of him everywhere?"

I bowed my head. "Forgive me," I said. "Your words have carried me away, astonished and astounded me. I forgot where I am. I forgot that I belong to this city of fire and destruction."

She patted my shoulder tenderly. "Patience. We have to learn the great lesson of patience."

"And hope ..." I said and felt the plea rise from deep inside me, changing within me. I turned to her. I wanted to tell her what great impact seeing her had wrought upon me, but ...

Need I say with words and images how this meeting

ended? Or do I let these ... dotted ... lines ... speak for themselves ...

The Green Bird

For a week now, that man has been sitting on the cement block facing my building. I do not know what winds blew him our way—a strange man. But who would dare ask these days? Who would query someone at the corner of a street in Beirut? Or in a bomb shelter? Or a hideout? Who would dare question anyone, whether man, woman or child? In Beirut these days one wouldn't dare ask questions like "Who are you? Where have you come from? Why are you here?" It would be like striking a match to the fuse of a bomb.

He has been sitting in that same place for a week now, immobile, not eating or drinking, nor even moving to answer the call of nature ... Or at least that is how it seems to me. I see him every time I walk in or out of my house—there he is.

How can I avoid looking at him? He is sitting there, facing the entrance. Not crouching in a corner, nor blending into a wall, nor squatting behind the trunk of what used to be a tree. Just sitting. Simply sitting on that concrete block—half a metal barrel, actually, filled with cement, used as a shield by a fighter at some point during the war. (Don't ask who poured the cement into the barrel, or when or for what purpose, for that is another long story. A nine-year-old story and growing older, its action taking place in this neighbourhood and that and the other ...) In any case, that is what he is sitting on—a makeshift stool he has turned into his makeshift headquarters, from which he darts his nervous glances.

This man seems to be living on the cement barrel. And I cannot avoid looking at him as I come and go. He's sitting in that strategic spot and ... watching me. Every time I open my door I see him watching me; every time I step out of the building, he's watching—or so I think. For I have not had the courage to make a move towards him, maybe get closer to him, introduce myself to him get to know him ... I wouldn't dare.

"Get to know him? Whatever for?" I ask myself as I slam the car door and take off as far away as possible from his piercing gaze.

Actually, that, I think, is what bothers me most about the man. His eyes. They are constantly searching, constantly roaming in all directions, in the direction of every noise or movement. His eyes seem as though they are bolting out of their sockets. And like a pair of nervous birds, they fly this way and that, dart up electric poles and down again, throw themselves against concrete walls in a bid to go through them. Then, realizing the impossibility of their attempt, they return to their place ... only to try once more.

Yes, it's his eyes that bother me. They are searching for the unknown, the unattainable. Always looking, seeking, searching. I question his motives, my doubts grow. Why has he chosen to take refuge in this place? Surely if he's lost something, is looking for someone, it would do him good to conduct his search walking around the city streets rather than ... Why here? Why does he not move from that spot?

Why? A huge why. An enormous question mark. It escapes me and hangs in the air and becomes part of the echoes around me. It obsesses me.

I could save myself this worry and gnawing curiosity and ask an alert neighbour. The one who lives at the intersection of other people's lives, recording every movement of their traffic. Or I could ask the building janitor. Yes! Great idea! And so simple—why hadn't I thought of it before?

Naturally, he answers my "why" with a smile that says he "has it all under control."

"Who? That man? He's one of the refugees, the displaced."

He waits for me to ask him the very obvious next question, "Where from? What part of the country has he run away from?"

He opens his book of war days, in which he's written newspaper headlines and news reports and radio broadcasts and analyses and rumours and stories that float in the air. "What does it matter?" he says finally. "He is a refugee and a stranger to this neighbourhood."

"Have you spoken to him?"

"Yeah, I did. The first day. He's from one of the really hard-hit areas. His people have taken refuge in the building facing ours—you know that, of course. There are twenty families. They have taken over all the empty apartments whose owners are in Europe." Sarcasm tinges his words.

He stops there to see whether I am satisfied with the information he has provided. Then he looks at me—a pregnant, knowing look and the same confident, all-knowing smile of a simple man, that says, "It's under control, I've got it all under control."

Blessed are the simple people, I think to myself. *Blessed are their simple, uncomplicated hearts ...* It is not easy in these times to be so simple-minded. Oh, how very difficult it is!

"So, madam ..." he continues, when he realizes that I am not going to ask any more questions. He continues because the story has been knocking on the walls of his conscience. It pushes him to tell it. "The man has a story, madam. No, a tragedy is what it is—"

I object to hearing this. Immediately I stop him. "He must have relatives. Family."

"Yeah, sure he does. They took the second floor in the building. But he refused to go up there, to stay there. The family is made up of—"

I interrupt him again, "It may be the shock of having to move. He'll soon get used to it and start leading a normal life ..." I move, I shuffle. I want to run away. I have no desire to hear what happened to the family, how many they are, how they live. I certainly don't want to hear the details of the tragedy that has befallen them. It has befallen the entire country. It has engulfed us all ... What good will the details do me? No, I certainly do not want to hear this story. "Do you hear me, man? What good are details once the whole is lost?"

"Ah, but some details are important. Some details carry within them the essence of the whole." My simple building janitor waxes philosophical, the words gushing out of him. He no longer awaits my questions or comments.

The door is half open and I try to leave, but he stands in front of it and points to the man sitting on his barrel, his voice an odd mixture of pity and mockery. "This man has lost his mind," he says. "And who would blame him, really. Man isn't made of stone, you know. Some tragedies are just too big for him. More powerful than he is. They destroy him."

Again I try to get away from the circle his words have drawn around me. But the door is half closed in front of me and the janitor has saddled his story and is preparing to take off on it.

"He keeps saying, 'He'll be back.' Do you know the story of the Green Bird? It's an old story. One of our forgotten legends told in the villages. 'I am the Green Bird/I walk with a swagger.' This is how it begins. You know it, the mother revives her son from the dead, rejuvenates his dried bones ..."

He quotes again, " 'My dear Mother/picks up my bones/places them in the marble urn ...' Do you remember? The other woman, the stepmother, had conspired against the beautiful young boy and killed him, and made of his body a feast for her friends. But his dead mother's soul revived him. It gathered his bones into a marble urn and nurtured them with drops of water until they came alive again!

"But her young son could not return as human flesh. He turned into a green bird and started haunting the other woman in dreams and wakefulness, hovering over her, plucking at her, reminding her of her crime, and that Judgement Day was near.

"This man here, he awaits the return of the green bird. He says he's afraid to close his eyes lest the green bird returns and he does not see it. He stays up all night, his eyes roaming all over the place. He's afraid to close his eyes and not see the green bird when he comes."

"Who is this green bird he talks about, anyway?" I hear myself asking the janitor, almost against my will. The story has conspired against me, and it hooks me, and I cannot free myself. "What is the green bird to this man?" I ask again.

My storyteller smiles, an almost mocking, nearly sad, slightly humorous kind of smile, and I think, *What is there to smile about? Didn't he say the story was tragic? Yes, but isn't there a saying that goes, the most tragic events are those that induce laughter?*

"It's his son, madam. His eldest son, his only son among five girls. He brought him up, educated him and put him through university and pinned all his hopes upon him. He sold everything he owned to put him through medical school. Yeah, he's a poor man, but he managed to put his bright son through university to become a doctor. Being bright, at least, is not the privilege of the upper classes alone, you know. God gave him a bright young boy, and through His divine guidance, the man educated the boy. He would have graduated from medical school at the end of the year. Then he would have been able to carry some of his father's burden. Maybe even put his sisters through school ... Who knows, one of them may even have been able to go to university herself! Who knows what the future would have held for the young man before the ..."

"Before what?"

I scream the question at him but he continues, calm, unperturbed. "Yes, madam ... Before that shell found him and ... 'he exploded.' "

The janitor shifts from philosophy to literature and waxes poetic. He draws the clearest of pictures for me and slaps me with it, using that one expression "he exploded," with all its literal connotations. I have certainly never heard it before—war slang, no doubt. And as he continues speaking, frame by frame the scene he describes plays out behind my eyes, and I am transported to a different time and place. The scene unfolds before me, running alternately in fast and slow motion—very slow motion.

"The shell surprised him as he was coming out of the bomb shelter. He had wanted to take advantage of the calm. He thought it was a truce or a ceasefire. He told his mother, 'I'll just go out for a minute and move the car to where it'll be safer.' That's when it surprised him. First one shell then the other ... They slammed him against the wall ... That's how they found him. His mother, his father, his sisters ... that's how they found him. Splattered across a wall in a hail of shrapnel and rockets and shells. It was raining bullets as the father gathered his son's remains into his bosom.

"One entire night the man sat in that pool of blood, his son's remains in his arms. One whole night. Then in the morning they had to pry what was left of the body from his arms in order to prepare it for burial. They had to pry it by force from his arms!

"He spent the entire night talking to his son, soothing

him. 'You are cold. The night is cold and dark. Listen to the thunder and the rain. My child is so cold. Leave him, leave him in my arms. I am keeping him warm.' The neighbours had to all work together to pry it away from him. Like prying open a clam shell to remove the precious pearl in order to bury it in the earth.

"Here he is now. He's lost his home and shelter and left the last of his rational mind in that pool of blood. If you go near him he'll ask you, like he asks everyone else, 'Have you seen him?' And you would say, 'Who?' And he'll tell you, 'The green bird, of course, who else? He's coming, don't you know. Come sit next to me. He'll be here any minute now.'

"He says that, and he doesn't care who you are or what your reaction will be to what he's saying. He may think you're his wife or one of his daughters. He may think you're there to wait, like he is. And he will just repeat those words to anyone who crosses his path. He'll ask them if they've seen it … ask them to sit quietly by him and wait … ask them to listen as he does, keeping his eyes open all the while … darting from one corner to the next … waiting … for the beloved green bird."

For the Sake of Her Eyes

The waves jostled and rolled, white caps that would soon reflect sleepy sunrays. Rising and levelling, their lapping was heard on the distant shore.

He swam within their folds. For hours he had been rowing, trying to cut a path towards a safe haven, a warm cove where he could throw himself on the sand, embrace it, hide in it.

A white sail rose suddenly over the water—a lone white sail hurled and pitched by the waves. Seagulls plunged towards it and Hamad heard their screeches as they scavenged and fought over food.

Long ago the sea was blue.

But the sea that spread open in front of him was colourless—"Water is colourless, tasteless, odourless." He repeated this sentence that had stuck in his memory from his school days.

He continued to swim and row. He knew he had to reach the distant shore before dawn, but the waves were growing heavier, engulfing him instead of carrying him on their crest.

The sea was blue.

His own sea, the Mediterranean. Why had they named it in Arabic the "white sea," when it alone, among all the seas and oceans of the world, was a pure, dark blue? Blue as her eyes.

As her eyes had been in happier times. In the times of hurried meetings when he had visited her in her father's home. In the times when they had stood under the vines and watched the sun set, the migrating birds, and the changing colours of the trees as they donned their autumn finery. He heard a whispering within him speak to her, "You will see me soon, Hanan. Do not worry. Hold on to the purity of the colour blue."

He opened his heavy lids, feeling as though they had been sealed together. He had sunk into a deep exhausted sleep. He was exhausted from paddling through an endless sea.

His gaze took in the darkened expanse around him. He felt his body, his clothes, his hair. All were dry. He was no longer at sea. He was on his soil, his body joined with it, stretched atop it as it hugged him with the arms of a gentle mother.

Like a ray of heavenly light, reality opened to him. He was back from a successful mission. But he had been injured along the way. He wondered where he could be. Tranquillity spread its wings around him as the world surrendered to sleep once again, and the cool breezes caressed his face.

He remembered his friend, Zayyan. They had returned together. Where was he? Could Zayyan have gone ahead of him, or had he, too, surrendered to sleep?

A warrior should not sleep. How had he slept?

He buried his finger in the wound at his side and found it deeper than he had first thought. That, then, was the reason. He had bled into a deep sleep.

And Zayyan. Had he been hit, too? Or was he lost in this dark, fearsome night? Or was he ... ? The thought ran like a shiver through his mind.

The heaviness in his lids threatened to drown him in numbing, enticing sleep. He tried to keep them open, tried to sit up straighter, but his world whirled around, and he nearly lost consciousness.

He groped at the darkness around him until his hand came upon a rock. He crawled toward it and rested his back against it. He was bleeding profusely, but could feel no pain. He could have continued to make his way back if it weren't for the rumbling sounds and the giddiness in his head. The hole in his side must be closed.

He tore off his sleeve and bunched it against the wound. And the rumbling ceased. The rumbling had been coming from his wound; he had imagined the noise to be the breaking of waves.

He hesitated before feeling the ground beneath him. But his hand was quicker than his mind, and with a will of their own, his fingers probed the damp soil and the sticky fluid. He had bled profusely into the silence of the black night and the loneliness of this place, without even knowing it, without even a star as witness.

If only she were near him. Hanan would not have left him this way, under the open skies. She would have taken care of him, defended him ... defended him ...

In spite of the weariness in his body and soul, his lips opened in a smile as he remembered the way she had attacked Abul'izz, the company leader. She had been carrying a thick stick in her hand at the time too.

He had been so taken aback by her action. He had thought her an angel descended from the heavens until that incident. He could not believe his eyes—in that moment his Hanan had turned from an angel into a fierce tigress and had attacked the big man.

He tried to erase the memory from his mind, but her face haunted him, in all its love and gentleness, as she looked tenderly down upon him and wiped away the weariness of his journey. He heard her ask, "How long will you be? No, no, don't answer that. Just remember that I will be waiting for you."

The darkness grew heavier and his eyes roamed like a pair of dizzy moths, crashing into walls.

Suddenly, he saw her coming to him out of the heart of

darkness, her hand extended to touch his fevered brow, and he heard himself saying, "Why did you do that, Hanan? Why did you behave that way?"

"It was for your sake ... Don't you know that?"

"But Abul'izz is my leader, and he can dismiss me anytime."

"But he insulted you ... I was afraid he might hit you ..."

"You misunderstood, my naive lily. It was merely an argument. I have a sharp tongue myself, as you know."

"But he was interfering in our affairs. He objected to our relationship."

"I tell you again, he is my leader and I have to obey him."

"Yes, but that doesn't apply to me ..." She choked on her words and he saw the crystal drops gather in her eyes and roll down her cheeks. She lowered her head and stared at the ground so he would not be able to see her weakness."

Those sweet moments, how could he ever forget them? How could he erase from his memory the way Abul'izz had backed away, taken by surprise. Ah, Hanan, how sweet and naive you are. Hold on to your purity and to the clarity of your blue eyes.

He'd had to apologize to his commander for the way she had behaved. He'd had to work twice as hard to qualify for the mission after that. The missions were the reason he had joined the unit, become one of the fedayeen.

Abul'izz was an intelligent young fellow, with a kind heart. He knew Hamad well and appreciated his loyalty and his zeal. That was what Abul'izz had told him. He had said also that he was reprimanding Hamad out of concern. He was afraid Hamad would weaken before love and lose his enthusiasm for combat, and leave the battle vanquished.

"I thought you knew me better, Abul'izz. After today I

will no longer need to explain myself. The scar of the open wound in my side will speak for itself," he said aloud.

And Hanan, how does he remember her? How can he forget her? Her face is with him everywhere he goes. It had never left him throughout his mission. How he had remembered 'Antar bin Shadad, the legendary hero of chivalry and romance. How he had wanted to embrace the sabres and grenades and all manner of explosions, for the sake of her eyes.

He felt truly like the incarnation of 'Antar. What would stop him from being the 'Antar of his battalion?

His love for Hanan doubled his enthusiasm and tempted him. It tempted him to self-sacrifice and battle. Tempted him to self-deprivation that his soul might live on.

He had completed his mission successfully. He and Zayyan had succeeded in blowing up an enemy ammunition dump, in silencing thousands of bullets, destroying hundreds of bombs and explosives with poisonous shrapnel. They had succeeded in saving the children of their country, the elderly and the incapacitated, the women and the pretty young girls like Hanan.

Hanan's father had been incapacitated. A poor, kindly man, he was. Everyone in the village knew that Salem Bittar was an obliging, kind-hearted man. One day he had suffered a stroke that nearly took his life. The village doctor had not been there, nor was he in the nearby village and Hanan had been frightened. She had run out of the house, screaming for help. He had been the first to heed her call. A distressed young woman, how was he not to answer her call for help? She was as beautiful as a lavender dawn bursting forth from behind the summit of Mount Haramoun.

He had accompanied her to her home without asking permission from his leader and he had used his experience and expertise to save the old man.

Abul'izz had not objected. But the father's recuperation became the cause of Hamad's illness, an illness that had affected him in the very depths of his heart. He had not excused himself from his battalion but had tried to tend to his "wound" whenever he had some free time.

"Abul'izz, what do you say to a lonely young woman of eighteen, living alone with an ill, elderly father, in a home that had lost a mother's warmth? And you a young man who lives under the open skies, sleeps upon the earth, with a rock for a pillow and anxiety for a blanket. You a person who lives for hope and the love of country and the sacrifice of all that is dear to save it. You, whose blood runs warm and whose heart beats strong. What do you say to eyes that, every time they leave you, take away with them the colour of the sea and sky and the promise of forbidden fruit? What do you do when you are no more than a weak human?"

Yes, he thought, *I told Abul'izz, "I am weak in front of her, my brother." I admitted that. From the moment we sat together by her father's bed, when she had given herself up to her pain and loneliness and sadness, alone with no one to protect her, I asked myself, What if the old man dies and she is left alone? What would she do, where would she go? She is not betrothed, she has no brother to look after her.*

All those were my thoughts as we sat by her father's bed, each of us too embarrassed to lift our eyes from the floor. I, because I did not want to disobey my command and take advantage of the situation, and she because she did not want to defy the customs of our society.

But when my visits became more frequent she was the first to lift her eyes and look at me. She thanked me, tears drowning her eyes in a deep blue. "You have become dearer to me than a brother," she murmured.

I told Abul'izz, "What do you expect a young man to do when presented with such a scene? What else can he do but take her in his arms, kiss her soft mouth and eyes and feel the warm body pulsing trustingly beneath his touch. Yes, I went that far before the warning bells rang in my head, "Remember, you are a stranger. You are not here in search of love."

And I ran away. Cowardly, weakly, I freed her from my hold and left the house, never looking back.

But the temptation was stronger than myself. The man in me conquered the hero, and her home became the only oasis in the desert of my life. And so I confessed all to Abul'izz. He thought for a long time before looking at me and saying, "Tomorrow you will receive your transfer orders from this company."

I shuddered as though touched by a live wire. "I beg of you, do with me what you will, but don't send me away from her."

He answered angrily, "A man like you is no good in battle."

"I will prove to you the opposite …"

He let me stay after extracting from me a promise that I would never see her again.

I accepted my punishment reluctantly, until the day I weakened and disobeyed the orders. Abul'izz found out from the comrades whom I was supposed to meet, and he followed me to her house. That was when our argument grew heated. She had been listening quietly to what was being said. Then suddenly she jumped out of her chair, left the room and returned with a thick stick.

"I will not allow anyone to interfere in our affairs …"

And to whom was she addressing these words? To my commander.

I jumped up to calm her, putting on a smile that I hoped would break the ice which had come into Abul'izz's glare. But what she did cost me dearly.

I knew at that moment that I would be transferred and that it would be a long time before I would see her again. But my departure would be for her sake, for the sake of her eyes, and I would return a hero that she would be proud of.

We left her home in silence. I with my head bowed, like a guilty student, and Abul'izz behind me. He was the first to speak, "You will leave early tomorrow morning to join another company. I will give you a certificate of good conduct because you are one of my best men. But I am unable to cure your weakness."

The next day, as he said good-bye to me in front of his tent, he whispered, "Do not feel ashamed of your weakness, we are all human. But discipline comes first for us."

May God keep you, Abul'izz.

∞

He gathered his smile from his lips and face, and felt his side for his wound. He tried to remember his location when he and Zayyan had been shot at.

He and Zayyan had already crossed the area that was heavily guarded when the sounds of explosions had come to them. They had started counting them until they could no longer count, and the explosions took on the urgency and frequency of terrified heartbeats. He could not remember what had happened after that. The echoes of explosions had filled his ears and he no longer heard the bullets that were aimed at them. He must have thought them an extension of the explosions from the munitions dump.

Now here he was, wakening in the midst of this terrible darkness, unable to rise ... He must rise ... at any cost, no matter how painful.

He must get up and continue his flight, he told himself. Or cover the distance, crawling on his stomach. He must reach his destination before dawn, before the enemy would be able to detect him.

But what about Zayyan? Should he leave without him? How would he be able to find him?

He listened intently for footfalls or the sound of crawling, or even a lung exhaling breath into the wilderness. Silence enveloped the place, calm spread over the universe.

He wondered what hour of the night this was. He tried to discern the answer from his wrist watch but found that it had stopped. His only guide was his compass needle.

He followed it, crawling on his stomach, one hand on the opening at his side.

What distance separated him from the men of his company? How far was the border? These were questions asked as though from a distance of a thousand years. Where were the rest of the company? Could he reach them? The questions crowded him, adding to the pounding and the dizziness.

He thought that the best he could do would be to stop asking questions and to keep on going until the dawn rose, to distance himself as far as possible from enemy territory. They should not capture him ... dead or alive. Especially not dead, or they would mutilate his body as they had done with those of his friends a week ago.

He would crawl until he could greet the dawn in friendly territory, away from the enemy's reach. This was his dream of the moment, his goal—he would achieve it and rest. He would find the same peace he had found upon deciding to join the guerrillas and sacrifice himself for his country.

He had been in his third year in medical school when he awoke to the call of the land, and heard the voice that called on him by name. "What are you doing here, Hamad?" it had said. "The world is full of doctors and scientists. None of them has been able to rescue your people from the misery and despair that gnashes at their hopefulness." His sense of pride, his high-minded idealism were stimulated; the rush of blood in his veins at the sound of the call had made him remove his white doctor's robe and don army fatigues.

His mother had protested. His professors had interfered. His father had remained silent. He had left his home with no word of good-bye.

And now he was going back to them. Back to her, crawling on one side, the side that was not hit by enemy bullets.

Go back to where, Hamad? Between you and the dawn

is an indeterminate distance. Your body is too weary to carry you. And this land is your land. She is the lover you held in your arms, the mouth you kissed, the tears you washed yourself in, the sweet breath that engulfed you. She is the fragrance that has embedded itself in your pores, the blood that flows in your veins and demands more love and more sacrifice.

Listen, Hamad. Listen to her whisper in your ear.

"Come, my beloved. Come closer to me. Bond with me, become one with me. Stretch your body inside my veins, unite with me ... unite with me ... unite with me ..."

Hamad opened his eyes to see the terrible darkness become a blinding light, robbing him of sight. The land and the mountains became a white cloud, light and flirtatious, tickling his brow, caressing his eyelashes and his lips.

He experienced an ecstasy he had never felt before. He was lying next to his beloved. His body was one with hers, sleeping like a child intoxicated by its mother's milk.

"Come to me Hanan ... Come to me so I can hold you. Parting brings such pain and sorrow. Parting is loneliness and trepidation awaiting the next meeting, and holding you brings my soul back to my weary body."

At dawn, his body was stretched out on an incline that rarely met a footfall. His face was to the ground, his limbs akimbo as though trying to hug the earth. His wound bled softly, the viscous liquid whispering joyously as it seeped into the ground, quenching the insatiable thirst of his land.

Is This A True Story?

I have tried so many times to tell my story to others but I have been unsuccessful. I do not know if my readers will give me a chance, or if they will turn their backs on me, just like the child I had been talking to.

I was sitting next to him, and he was looking up to me like children often will look up to their elders. And he *wanted* a story. In fact he *insisted* on a story.

"I will tell you a story," I said.

"Is it a true story?" he asked enthusiastically.

"Oh, absolutely, one hundred percent true." His eyes sparkled with anticipation in his smooth pink face.

But as soon as I started speaking he stood up, objecting, "This is not a true story."

He would not give me a chance to finish telling it, to prove my good intentions. I watched as he walked to the door and closed it behind him. Keen disappointment replaced my happiness as I watched him sitting beneath a tree, toying with an insect that had just emerged out of the belly of the earth.

I told myself, in an attempt at consolation, "He is only a child. And what do children know of the treasures we hold for them in our hearts?"

But when I tried to tell the same story to his older sister, she had no more patience than he. "This is so old-fashioned. My generation really doesn't care for these stories."

"But it's a true story. Don't you care to know about a strange incident that's actually true?"

She answered me mockingly, "And what is truth? Do you know?"

"Well, it's anything we can feel and touch and know using our physical senses."

"That's only your opinion. The truth is very different from your definition of it."

"Child, listen to me," I said. "I am not talking about absolute truth. I am just telling you that this is a true story—that is, truth limited to this story."

"Or what you believe to be the truth. You have no right to impose your idea of truth on anyone, especially someone not of your generation, who thinks differently from you."

I received her stabs with both palms open. Then I stood and started to walk away.

"I see you are running away," she called out.

"Merely to search for someone who will hear my story. There must be someone who is interested in it."

∞

I knocked on the door of one of my closest neighbours. She greeted me with enthusiasm, in her kitchen apron. "Welcome, welcome. What a pleasant surprise."

"I thought I'd surprise you with a visit and a story."

"A story?"

"Let's just say it's a story that happened to someone."

"And how do you know about it?"

"I was a witness to it."

"Ah, well then, it is no longer a story," my neighbour said.

"How can you say that without even hearing what I have to say? What is a story then?"

"I can say that because you say you were a witness to this incident. Therefore you are here to present an eye witness account and not to tell a story. Anyway, do I know the people involved?"

"I don't think so. But what do you care? The incident is what is important, not the characters in the story."

"Come on then, either tell me who the heroes of this story are, or ..."

"Or leave?" I asked

Her social graces won over, and she said, "God forbid! Come in, we'll have a cup of coffee together. I am baking a beautiful date and walnut cake. A few minutes and it'll be out of the oven. Just wait until you taste it."

∞

"Thank you," I said much later, "for the delicious coffee and cake and your hospitality. And thank you for not giving me a chance to tell you my story. It has given me the opportunity to think about it even more."

∞

But words tap against the walls of the chest seeking passage to the lips, like fingers tapping on a closed door. Like a child who's been promised an outing or new clothes for a special occasion, my words sit within me, anxious and edgy, waiting to be set free. Like a travelling salesman with unsaleable wares, I had to go out and comb the street in search of a customer who would buy my story.

∞

At the corner of the street, I saw a frail old man in worn and tattered clothing, sitting on a flat rock with his face in his hands, his eyes fixed on a point between his feet.

I have found my target, I thought. *Here is a poor old man with nothing to do. The ideal person to listen. I'll just approach him and tell him my story.*

It was evening and people were hurrying by, carrying bags and parcels, whipped by hunger, prodded by the strain of their day, and weighed down by exhaustion. None of them looked our way. *I can now isolate my "victim,"* I thought, *surround him, block his escape routes, cut off his breathing space and tell him my story.*

"Good evening, old sir," I greeted him. But he did not raise his head from his hands nor glance at me.

The man must be deaf, I thought to myself. *I'll just move closer and he'll be able to see me.* I did, but he did not look up at me.

I thought, *What if he is blind? I'll shake him by the shoulder and see.* He did not move and I felt as though my hands had touched a cold, inanimate body.

A statue, maybe. That was what I thought until I saw the blood flowing from his right temple.

The man is dead. I must get away from here. I must run away before anyone sees me, before they accuse me of this crime.

But should I? Is it right, humane, to leave this man in this deserted corner, now that night has started falling—to turn my back on him? No. I shouldn't do this. It is my duty to tell the police about what I have seen and what I know.

But what do I know? What have I seen?

∞

"Yes, I saw the blood trickling."

"How long have you known this man?" asked the police officer in a tone that conveyed his suspicions of me.

"A few minutes."

"What prompted you to approach him?"

"I wanted to tell him a story."

"A story? Are you making fun of me? Tell me the truth. What was your motive for approaching a man you do not know?"

"This is the truth. I have a story to tell. A true story. I started telling it to a child but he ran away. I tried to relate it to his sister, but she mocked me. I knocked on my neighbour's door and found her submerged in kitchen duties. So I went out into the street and he was the first ..."

"The first what?"

"Well, the first to attract my attention. He was sitting in a corner, his head in his hands, staring at the ground in front of him. I felt he would be the ideal person to listen to my story."

"So you approached him?"

"I approached him."

"And then?"

"I greeted him."

"And … ?"

"He didn't answer."

"So?" prompted the police officer.

"I stood in front of him so he would see me."

"And did he?"

"No. He didn't lift his eyes up. That's what made me think he might be blind."

"And so what did you do?"

"I reached out and shook him by the shoulder."

"Did he respond?"

"No. His shoulder was rock-hard and I …"

"And you what?"

"I was stunned when I saw blood trickling down his right temple."

"Was there no reason for the blood?"

"I didn't say that!"

"Then what are you saying? What, does the man's head leak like the municipality's rotting water pipes?"

"Yes, yes. And that's what stunned me so much. That's why I came to you."

"To tell me how stunned you are?"

"To tell you …"

"… The story?"

"Yes."

"And this one is different from your first story."

"Well, yes, of course!"

"But like the other one, it is also a true story?"

"Certainly."

"And you are the only one who knows the truth? The only witness?"

"I object."

"To your own testimony?"

"No, no. I am objecting to what you said. I don't know the truth."

"Which truth are we talking about now? The first true story or the second?"

"Well, like the girl told me, there is another truth, a different truth ..."

"But the girl was not with you when you had gone out on the street."

"Right!"

"So there was no one but you as a witness."

"Witness to what?"

"The truth. You will be detained for questioning."

"Sir, you have to listen to my story. It's a true story. I didn't make it up, not one letter of it. You have to hear it."

"Tomorrow. In court. You can tell the judge tomorrow the whole story, every letter of it ..."

Looking for Randa

Sami's telephone call on that autumn evening was totally unexpected. I knew he had been out of the country for years. He resided abroad permanently, and insisted he would not return before the war ended.

That was what Randa had told me when she had related her domestic problems. Sami had wanted her to leave the country and accompany him, with their three children, to Paris.

Sami is a sensitive man. He has no stomach for wars. He loves his family to the point of worship and cannot abide the thought of them being in danger. And danger is everywhere here; if you do not seek it out it seeks you, crashes through your door like an obnoxious guest.

Randa had given me some idea about the situation between her and Sami. It had finally ended in a screaming match, after which the man had packed his bags and left, saying he was never coming back.

Randa is stubborn. In fact, I could never understand her stubbornness. Her husband had been transferred to Paris. Many a wife had followed her husband to new work locations; some to Paris or London, or any city in the East or West where the men could find work, and where the family would have a safe home.

Randa loves her three children dearly and cares immensely for their safety. Moreover, she has no commitment to career, or any relationships that would keep her in Beirut.

I suppose rationality and reasoning cannot explain one's attachment to land and country. Nor can one prove how one's body and soul are an extension of one's surroundings. That, at least, was what I told myself when I became incapable of understanding Randa's behaviour. But I must admit that there were times when I doubted such explanations and accused her of having ulterior motives for wanting to stay here. I accused her of hiding the true reasons for her refusal to leave the country.

Failing that, I had explored the philosophical reasons and deep-rooted psychological grounds for her insistence on staying here. I had reasoned that she had become addicted to living with danger—the constant threat, the excitement—and would rather stay than migrate to a normal but boring life. However, I never understood her reasons with any certainty. Randa is an emotional person who keeps her thoughts and feelings under tight rein. She rarely opens the door to intimacy.

I was surprised Sami would call me after such a long silence. It had been four months since the Israeli forces had invaded Lebanon, nearly two months since they had invaded West Beirut. We had returned from our diaspora.

"We" refers to the last inhabitants of the city, those who did not emigrate in spite of reasons, real or imagined, that might compel them to do so. It refers to those whose homes, businesses and shops were destroyed. And who have returned to rebuild and resume.

We felt, as we looked out of our ruined homes and collapsed balconies, that we had been unified by catastrophe. We were drawn together by familiarity. The strange mood and an eagerness to rebuild heightened our need to challenge disaster, like no previous time.

I was one of those people. It was natural that reconstructing my home and everything around it would be uppermost on my mind. I was thus preoccupied when the phone rang and I heard Sami's voice on the other end of the line.

"Hello ... Muna. How are things?"

"Sami? Where are you all?"

"I am here. But tell me, what do you know of Randa?"

"*Randa?*" I had not meant to cry out.

I had thought Randa was in Paris. Or at least that was where I had hoped she had gone when I thought about her during the seige of the capital, when the fighting had reached its apex and everyone was suffocating. When I called to ask about her and the children the phone was never answered and its hollow ringing echoed in my ears. I had harboured no doubt that Randa, unable to stand the pressures of Beirut, had taken her children and left, as had thousands before her.

Out of nowhere her husband was now asking me what I knew of Randa. Trying to calm my turbulent thoughts, I said, "Maybe she's staying with one of her friends. You see communication had been cut off and the roads were impassable because of sand-bags and sand dunes. Some people are still huddled in safe places. Don't worry too much about it ... She might have taken the children to a safe area away from lines of fire."

I hoped I sounded convincing. Especially since Randa and Sami's home is located near one of the areas that had seen the fiercest fighting. Most of the houses and buildings in that neighbourhood had been destroyed. Their apartment had, by some miracle, escaped total destruction. I discovered that when I had first made my rounds of the area after I returned. I, too, had wanted to check on Randa and the children.

I had parked my car in front of their building and looked up toward the seventh floor. I was quite elated to see no signs of fire or destruction from where I stood. Many of the apartments below and above theirs had received direct hits, and some had been burnt.

But, Randa, where could she be?

Sami, was still on the other end of the line, his voice desperate. "But when did you last see her?" he asked.

It was extremely difficult to answer that question. I did not want to lie to my friend's husband. At the same time I wanted to help him, to stave off his rising panic. So I answered, trying to put the blame on my own neglect, "I left Beirut before her," I said. "I was unable to get in touch with her. When things got really bad in our neighbourhood, we had to go up to the mountains. But tell me, did you ask any of the neighbours about her?"

"Neighbours?" he asked, resignation in his voice. "There are no neighbours. There's no one in the building. Even the cockroaches have left."

I was confused, riddled with anxiety. My conscience hammered at me scoldingly, *You should have told him* ...

But I am not even sure she went there, I answered my conscience.

She told you. A few days before the invasion of Beirut she told you about it ...

Yes, she had called me. "Muna," she had said, her voice tremulous, horror-stricken, "I don't know what I want anymore. I don't know what to do. Sami wants me to leave immediately, and you know how I feel about leaving—"

I had interrupted her fiercely, "This is no time to stand on principles. You have to protect your children, they are your responsibility."

"Yes, of course, I know that. That's what frightens me so much. Where do you want me to take them? I am not going to Paris. And here there isn't a spot that is not threatened by the shelling, everywhere, on all fronts, from the land and the sea and the sky."

I really had tried to help her make a decision. "You could go to your house in the mountains," I had said.

"No. No ..." she had cried out. "The mountains, too, are threatened. I have no choice but to take them to the sea palace."

I had laughed in spite of myself. I had no doubt Randa

was joking, trying to relieve the sombre mood, but her voice had brought back the seriousness of the conversation.

"I am not joking. I'll take them to the sea palace. We'll just stay there until the war is over."

That was when I had raised my voice at her, "You *are* crazy! The battleships' shelling is concentrated on the coast. What's *wrong* with you?"

"Yes," she had said, "You're right. But the shelling from the battleships will not reach the sea palace."

"How is that?" I had mocked.

She had answered me earnestly, "Because it's beyond suspicion."

I had not argued with her, or offered any opposing opinions. I knew the shelling was indiscriminate. If it gets you you're dead, and if it doesn't, you're just lucky. I had also learned important lessons from the war: never to be too generous with my advice; never to tell people what to do and where to go; never to be too sure of myself, too confident of my beliefs. The war had stripped all the self-confidence we spent years building. It had wrenched all certainty from within us like a gusting wind wrenches delicate saplings up by their roots.

Besides, what did I know about this sea palace except its name? And it was a name that Randa had made up. Up until that very moment I had thought the palace merely a figment of her imagination. My friend has quite an imagination, and all manner of stories pour out of her. She had come to me one day with the story of this sea palace. I have been living by the sea for nearly twenty years and had never heard anyone speak of it before.

"Of course you haven't," she had said. "It's unknown. The only people who know about it are a band of old fishermen."

"And is it … er … located in the middle of the sea? On, say, one of the islets?"

She had laughed at my naivete. "Of course not. It's

under the sea. Under the centuries-old rocks," she had said, pointing to the giant rocks jutting out of the sea.

I had shouted at her, "A palace? Under the rocks? You remind me of fairy tales, of Aladdin and his magic lamp."

"I am introducing you to the sea. Why don't you come with me and I'll show you the palace?"

Naturally I never went. I kept postponing the visit.

Although I had no interest in her bizarre palace, Randa had never let an opportunity go by without telling me about it.

"No, it's not a cottage like you seem to think. It's not even a cave formed by erosion. It's an actual palace. It may have belonged to a king at one time. You get there through a long corridor, then you go down a few steps to reach the front entrance. It is always open. But it is protected from the strong sea current, and you can feel the gentle breeze and hear the whisper of the waves. As soon as you enter, you find yourself inside a huge hall. Around the hall are smaller rooms carved out of the rock. You could live in these rooms for months, even years, and no one would be able to find you."

I had listened to Randa talk, my mind objecting and arguing. "That's a pleasant dream. But this is not the safe haven you imagine it to be."

"It *is* safe," she had said, shaken. "The way it's made, its location, its secrecy, make it safe."

"What about intruders, thieves? Haven't they found it yet?"

"It belongs to the fishermen. They told me about it ten years ago. Since then we've been friends. They're a clique of seafarers, and they accept no outsiders."

"Oh, but of course, they accepted you," I had said, exasperated.

"Yes, they did. I am a seafarer too, all year round. Oh, I wish you would come with me one day and then you'd believe what I am telling you."

I had no interest in going with her—I felt no enthusiasm for her palace. Finally, I had relegated the whole conversation to oblivion. As the situation worsened, fear, anxiety, a hail of rockets and shells took over our days, and the sea palace had never again crossed my mind.

Under a veritable downpour of artillery, we had left our home after it became the target of direct hits. We drove aimlessly, entering one alley, exiting onto another and returning to the starting point. The roads had been transformed into confusing circles by sand barricades piled high on every street.

I will not detail our escape except to say what everyone who lived through our barbaric war has felt: we shrunk. We felt so insignificant, our entire universe shrunk to the size of an egg.

That is why I was cut off from all news of Randa and I could no longer get in touch with her. And the long days of fire and annihilation had caused a rift among the closest of people.

After the guns had fallen silent and we were able to return to our homes, to pick up the bleeding pieces of our life, the first thing I did was to check on friends and neighbours. Randa was one of those. She was not home. I also found no one in her neighbourhood to ask about her. I thought she had left with the convoys of the sorrowful and dejected who had fled the death that stalked their doorsteps.

I kept waiting for some word of her. I had no doubts at all that she had taken her children and gone to her husband; that she was safe, away from danger and death. I was convinced of that, and that was why I did not worry about her. And now here was Sami, on an autumn eve, four months after the Israeli forces invaded Lebanon, two months after they invaded Beirut ...

"What do you know of Randa?" he asked.

I stammered; the words ran away from me, the demons of doubt and fear assailed me, and my thoughts took me away, far away. I saw in my mind my friend and her three children squeezed into a hole in the rocks—a hole she calls a palace. The fighting had stopped a month ago, and if she had indeed gone into that hole in the ground she would have come out by now.

Apprehensions attacked me, like the assault of winged bats in a darkened cave, and a voice whispered to me, *If Randa were alive she would have been in touch with you.*

I closed my eyes and held my head in my hands and shook it, but the images would not leave me. I saw her tugging at her children, each one of them a little angel, telling them a story, speaking of her palace and all the surprises within it. And they followed her, awed, walking towards the adventure of a lifetime, believing what she told them, doubting nothing. She was their mother, she wanted only what was best for them; their health and safety.

She was telling them, "The palace will protect us. The fighting will no longer threaten us. Here we are in a safe haven, prepared for us specially by Mother Nature and the sea."

They accompanied her inside, crawling on their stomachs for the opening was too small, even for them. They continued to crawl, overwhelmed, for this is the first time they had played such a game. Once inside she lit a candle for them. They huddled in a corner, and on the shadowy light of the candle, they listened to the world above them tremble and quake.

Then I saw her in another scene. I saw the children, exhausted, using her lap for a mattress, as she bends over them to cover them with her body. And then I saw her rising in the morning to feed them. Pushing food down their throats like a female bird does with her offspring. She might have had some canned foods with her. Or maybe she found a cache of food in some part of her palace, left there by her friends the fishermen.

All I can say is, maybe. This is the only vision I have, and beyond it is a wall upon which all my doubts crash.

And Sami?

Poor, wretched Sami! He still expects an answer from me to put his mind at ease. And what else can I say?

We Are All Alright

Now I can write to you. Now that I have locked all the doors and secured the windows, I can hide my head in this little corner and write. There are only little openings left for the air that brings with it the smoke of smouldering fires, the thunder of explosions, and the screeching of the demons outside.

I write to you, my friend, to tell you that we are all alright. I pause at that last word, and I wonder, does it still have the same meaning as the old "alright"?

Don't interrupt me. Let me explode out of my age-old silence. I have overcome the silence in which your voice had drowned me. Your voice that came from a place unknown to me.

"I am calling from East Beirut. We have crossed the green line and arrived safely. We have nothing with us except our identity cards and the house keys."

Your voice sounded choked across the lines: *"I know, I know. I Can't waste time explaining. Can't speak with a silence that encloses the words. Can't describe feelings and heartbeats. Can't open the way to tears."*

Let me continue.

It was the third week of the war. The missives of death were dropping over your neighbourhood along the southern coast of Beirut. That phone call was the last I heard from you and of you, before the telephone lines were downed and all crossings closed. The sky rained fire and destruction and I had no way of finding out about you except through the news, or rather through what was not mentioned on the news bulletins.

I would wait for those rare times when the guns grew silent to go out on the balcony and look towards a horizon choked with black smoke. My eyes withdrew and my lips murmured supplications. What is left to us, we who live here in the throbbing heart of this city, but prayer and supplication?

I know the decision to purchase your house had been a mutual one made by you and your husband. You told me about that on our first meeting, remember? It was nearly a quarter of a century ago. We were both students at the American University. I was impressed by your maturity and your thirst for knowledge. Also, the gold band on your ring finger.

"Yes, I am married. I have three children and they all go to school," you said with such pride. "Life is a school with open doors, isn't it?"

I really had nothing to say, so you continued, "My husband is an engineer and I am a teacher. I am doing my post-graduate studies to get a doctorate. When, I don't know. But I am on my way."

You persevered. You received your doctorate and graduated at the same time as your eldest son. That was an important event for us. It was even written up in the newspapers. They made of you the symbol of the new woman in our society. The woman of unlimited ambitions.

Your husband, too, was building his ambitions. With steel and concrete. You chose that tranquil spot in the suburbs. "You know how I feel about peace and tranquillity," you said. "Here I feel I am part of the city, but separate from it at the same time."

But you remained in contact with all that was happening in the capital, especially cultural events, even though you were separated from its noise by gardens and jasmine trees.

The interior of the house, you had turned into a dream. In some areas it surpassed a dream. And I remember so well the time you introduced me to its rooms and balconies, and every nook and cranny of it. And especially that wonderful room, the library.

"This is my intellectual oasis," you said. In fact, it became an intellectual oasis for all of us, your friends. And your enthusiasm for travel opened a window onto the world for us. Wherever you went, you came back with precious books and films of historical and archaeological sights you had visited. And you would tell such stories about your adventures in your unique way that transported us and almost made up for our inability to travel.

When last you called me, you were, as I have always known you to be, strong and optimistic and self-confident. You assured me saying, "We're not leaving the house whatever happens, we're staying here, we have a basement shelter and enough food to last us six weeks."

I did not put much weight on what you were saying. I did not tell you, not even jokingly, about the meeting that day I had chosen to miss, a meeting with the other tenants in my building to organize a shelter.

I did not want to speak to you of my cowardice, my pathological fear of shelters that had turned into a tenacious phobia. I would see everyone around me running to the shelters while I remained nailed to my spot, unconcerned with time or space—surrendering my life to the fates, believing whole-heartedly in the popular philosophy about dying only when your time comes.

I never told you about any of those things. I simply wished you safety and hung up. And the very next day the telephone lines connecting your neighbourhood to the world were cut off because of the intensity of the shelling, and I had no news of you except what I could get from the frequently broadcast news bulletins.

You can imagine my happiness at your latest call, telling me of your safety. And I forgot in my happiness to ask you the few essential questions I had prepared during my long hours of silence, when I sat thinking about absent friends and loved ones. I was so taken aback by the hesitation in your normally proud voice. I was shaken by your broken spirit and the tears in your words.

I don't remember ever seeing you cry in public, not even in the saddest of situations. You were always strong, controlling your emotions with the same willpower that built your personality, your home and your family.

I could not stand hearing your tears and so I said, scolding you, "This is no time for tears. We cannot cry now."

But I realized how superficial my words were and I grew silent, listening to you mumble, "I have to tell you everything ... everything. But for now let me give you an idea of what it was like.

"We left under a hail of rockets while fires burned in neighbouring buildings, in warehouses and gardens. The sky was a showcase of modern artillery; the inventions of the civilized minds. Roads were devoid of human or animal life. Even the stray dogs had abandoned their haunts. We were the only ones left in the entire area. But my husband and I remained, steadfast in our determination. We leaned on each other for support.

"We spent such long, dark nights in the shelter, in our basement, listening from our black depth to the roar and surge, the raging and storming and threatening noises that left no room in your mind for anything else. We thought our shelter had enough protection from their evil. Until the air attacks started. I am still looking for suitable adjectives to describe those. Rockets rained from the sky, flew across the waters, dropped down from the hills. We felt the ground shake underneath us; the foundations of our home, strong enough to carry ten storeys, shifted and swelled beneath us, roaring like the breakers of July, growing nearer, crashing into our ear drums, slapping at the window panes and shattering them around us. A huge building collapsed, the flames rising from within to meet those falling from the sky. It was as though whoever had designed this last round of the war had decided it would end in a frightening crescendo, like a demented symphony.

"It was then that we were carried across the room and flung into a wall by an explosion. And when we opened our eyes we were surrounded by flames, licking at us from above and we knew that we would die in minutes if we did not leave our 'shelter.' Outside the shelling continued, relentless, the bombs stitching the earth. We burst out the door in search of a breath of air unscorched by the fire and smoke.

"We knew we had to make a decision about where to go, but we didn't. The building in front of us was felled and split in two and the decision was made.

"I looked at my husband and his eyes said, 'We have to leave now. Our home can no longer be saved.'

"And I said to him, gathering some hope to myself, 'By some miracle it will be saved.' We ran to the car.

"I quelled the doubts that crept into my conscience. Why did a miracle not happen when the neighbours' house blew up? Why did a miracle not happen when the neighbourhood went up in flames? When the women and children were killed? When the young boys and girls, the orphans and the handicapped were blown up? Why?

" 'Why' followed me throughout, as we made our way out of a home that held the dearest, fondest moments of our lives, that held our life. We passed through bent roads and crooked streets; went through craters and ditches; passed the barricades of the warring parties; went by angry eyes like poisoned lances; and walls of hatred rising up at the borders that divided Beirut into two unequal parts. And when we reached the safe area between the two sides, we realized what price we had paid to save our lives.

"I will leave you with this for now. I'll tell you the rest when we meet again."

As for me, my friend, I am still crouched in my little corner, writing to you from behind closed doors and barricades of fear and anxiety, and roadblocks that open and close according to the will of others. Between the opening and closing seep a few drops of water, a handful of food. And maybe, just maybe, a few items of news will be smuggled out to the world to tell of what is happening here, of the forgotten suffering in this part of the universe.

I tell you, my friend, as pain carves new pathways into my heart, that the fire that devoured the homes in your neighbourhood is steadily approaching, with giant steps, threatening our buildings. As we sit in little pockets within the city, waiting for it, or maybe not waiting for it, just trapped and cornered by this war while the world watches from afar our suffering.

When will the fire reach us?

I don't know. I also don't know whether this letter I write by the light of a candle will die as we do, leaving only tears behind.

I tell you, I am not sure whether this letter will ever reach you, but I am writing it to tell you, anyway, that we are all alright.

Peace be with you.

Our Daily Bread

We would sit together and talk about the war, Sana' and I. Sometimes pessimism and hopelessness descended upon us, covering us like a tent. Then we would grow silent, as though cement blocks and sand bags had blocked the way for words. Our words sank and hid within the depths of our throats.

But in untroubled times of tranquillity, we would sit around and analyze the situation, in our simple way that depended on theories.

At the end of one of our sessions, Sana' stood up, and with a mocking smile on her face and a sigh from the depth of her heart, she said, "And now that we've put to rest all the unresolved matters of the world and put an end to the war, I have to go back home and cook for my family."

And with a wink she added sarcastically, "You do know, of course, that a woman's role is not restricted to theorizing and finding political solutions and discussing philosophical matters. We have to cook and clean and take care of everything in order to deserve our title of real women!"

She threw out her words in a funny, endearing way, and took her leave of me in a loving manner. The war had not changed her, nor hardened her, as it had so many people.

Sana' had her own unique way of welcoming friends or bidding them farewell. She hugged warmly and affectionately. Without reservations, she poured all her love into them, and coated their hearts with her ever-present joy of life. She gave everyone around her a feeling of warmth and well being; a promise of better things to come in spite of the darkness of war, in spite of the walls of anger, hatred and resentment erected around us. She made us feel that the world she inhabited, and us with it, would always be alright.

Some time ago she came to visit me, after a forced absence that had lasted months. I hugged her, my heart soaring with the joy of seeing her again safe and sound, with the relief that she had—that we all had—made it out of our basement prisons, out of our damp and smelly shelters.

"I was afraid we would not meet again," I said to her, looking at the changes the war had wrought on her already slim figure. "I ... was ..." I choked on my tears.

She realized my words would drag us into the tragedy of what had happened. She jumped out of her seat and with a laugh she twirled around in a little dance to show she was still the same, then returned to her place, and laughed ... She laughed until her eyes filled with tears. That was Sana'. Always using laughter to mask the tears in every delicate situation, holding her smile up like a shield in the face of tragedy. And she often cried with laughter, but she never cried with pain or sadness.

That was Sana', sweet and unique and funny.

Then she and I sat and talked, just like we had always done in the days of peace and good living.

It was the first time we had seen each other after the invasion of Beirut. We did not talk much, for the sound of rockets and explosions still deafened us; the smell of fire and smoke burned our nostrils; and the names of victims filled the distance between us. After awhile we sat in silence—she smoking her cigarette and sipping her bitter coffee and I looking out at the remnants and rubble of the homes around us.

I tried to interrupt our silence and bring her back to the present. "Where to from here … ?"

She looked at me at length and said nothing.

I repeated my question, "When will salvation finally come our way, Sana'? Do you think we have reached the limit, that this is the beginning of the end?"

Again she looked at me, silently, and the silence filled more empty moments. I respected her feelings and withdrew into the hidden pockets of myself. There I saw a pencil moving of its own volition in the distance between us, drawing a caricature of our little session.

I shuddered. Then I started laughing out loud, bringing her out of her silence. She looked towards me and said, "I hope to God that only good things are making you laugh. What is so funny?"

Actually, I did not really know why I was laughing, for the situation was rather sad. Or was I crying, hiding my tears with laughter? I still do not know the meaning of my laughter at that time. I do not want to dwell on that confusing moment when everything around us had collapsed, and we were trying to reconnect the broken lines of friendship and human relations.

Yesterday she appeared anew, after a long absence outside the country. Her presence reminded me of a saying by an Indian philosopher, "Sometimes we see the face of God in the presence of our friends."

I was cooped up inside my house, walking through rooms empty save for the holes in the walls made by the flying shrapnel of continuous war. They were like slap marks on the face of memory. I no longer remembered what corner would provide me with some semblance of peace and tranquillity, in which to remember friends now scattered around the globe, who only yesterday had taken refuge in each others' hearts.

I lived in a circle of anxiety, the sounds of distant

artillery fire echoing around me. They coincided with sounds of sirens, speaking of yet more victims falling on every front, until the very earth groaned with the burden and the rocks crumbled from the weight. The radio stations still competed to get the terrible news out to their listeners.

Suddenly, Sana' arrived. She looked healthier than I had seen her before, her face had regained its colour. But when we embraced I could feel her tremble against me.

"Congratulate me on my narrow escape ..." she said, before I had a chance to ask her anything. "You could have been walking in your friend's funeral procession ... this morning."

I backed away from her and whispered, "May God send nothing but good!"

"Oh, no, it's only good," she said, mocking me. "A small explosion, is all. A booby-trapped car and it nearly ended my life."

"You?"

"Yes, me. What's so strange about it being me? How am I different from anyone else? Why not me ..."

"Tell me. Calmly tell me what happened," I interrupted.

"The explosion at the bank," she said. "Didn't you hear about it?"

"Of course, I heard about it. Once and twice and ten times."

"I was there!" she said quietly.

I cried out in disbelief, "There, there? At the bank, or on the road?"

"I was on the road, and I had just entered the building next to the bank. I heard the explosion as I was getting on the elevator. My ears still ring with the sound of it."

I had little to say, except to murmur the prayers that come automatically, as though they were my only salvation and my last shelter. "Thank God for your escape ..."

"It was luck," she said calmly, "I escaped injury, others

did not. It was just their turn and not mine. Next time might be my turn, who knows? We cannot afford to forget that for a single minute."

I tried to pull her out of the cloud of pessimism that had enveloped her. "Every day brings its own provisions. It is enough to deal with the evils one day at a time."

She watched me for awhile. Then without saying a word she walked to the front door. Quietly she opened the door and stood on the threshold for a few seconds. Then she disappeared out the door, leaving me with that strange confusion, the mysterious sensation one has when confronted with someone who "nearly left the land of the living." Someone who will never again be able to take life for granted; someone for whom the incident becomes an obsession, feeding on the mind and nurtured by the heart. It is as if that person had received a sign and the sign had been drawn invisibly on his forehead.

I do not remember what farewell she bade me. Except that she had murmured something about having work to do, having an important rendezvous to go to.

I prayed for her and followed the prayers with a thousand "God be with you's." And I returned to the nucleus of my home, my office. But before I opened my book and took up my pen, I turned on the radio. The news-flash music was on, the tune that makes hearts jump in a panic: "Here is the latest news flash on the situation." My blood turned to ice as I listened to the voice pant at the enormity of the news it was delivering: "A huge car bomb exploded a few minutes ago, resulting in a large number of casualties. We will keep you posted as more news comes in ..."

A few minutes ago! In that district? That's the same neighbourhood where Sana' lives. Did she go home? No, no ... she said she was going to an important rendezvous. She said she was busy.

I reached for the phone to dial her home number. It was impossible. The hotter the war situation, the colder the telephones become. No sign of life, no dial tone. Dead. Below zero temperature.

But *Sana'*! How do I get to her? Could she be among the wounded? Or one of the d... No ... no ...

The radio announcer again. With numbers and the names of victims this time. More than twenty killed and tens more injured. I listened carefully; an endless list of names. None of them Sana'. Maybe she had already passed that area before the explosion. Or maybe she took another route. She must have taken another route if she was going to that meeting of hers. But where ... ? Where was that meeting taking place? Why hadn't I asked her? What if she went home to change her clothes before going to the meeting? I should have asked her. Maybe ... What if ... ?

Doubt is a vicious killer. It always attacks when you're down. And once your defences have gone down you can only sink further into despair.

I spent the next few minutes in the shadow of my doubts, guessing. My only contact with the explosion was the needle on my radio moving from one station to the next, all of them delivering the same news to their listeners.

I was still in that state when my phone gave a strangled ring. I jumped on it, took up the receiver with trembling hands.

A stranger's voice on the other end said, "Mrs. Muna Al Ghazal?"

"Are you Mrs. Muna?" asked the voice again and only my lips answered that indeed I was, while in my head a devil rampaged.

"Yes, yes, that's me. And you are ... ?" He did not give me a chance to finish the question.

"I am Dr. Nouman, from the University Hospital ..."

"Dr. Nouman, yes. What is it? Why are you calling me?"

"I would like you to come to the hospital immediately.

Your friend indicated—before she—well, that her family was out of the country and that you are the person closest to her. Come immediately."

"No ... I don't know you, Doctor. You must have the wrong number. You know how the phones are these days. Besides, my phone is not even working, you couldn't have called me. You don't know me and everything is so mixed up, the telephone lines, the names, the numbers, the faces ... You dialled the wrong number, Doctor!"

∞

No ... no ... I won't believe it. Only a little while ago she left here, in perfect health and spirit. She told me she had escaped an explosion by a miracle. She came to tell me that.

She left saying she had an appointment. An important appointment. And I know her: she never breaks a promise. She never misses a rendezvous.

The Unspoken Word

I remember as one remembers a dream that may have been reality. I was there with a crowd of people. Some faces were familiar and others had never before crossed the paths of my memory. We were walking through a vast field, where neither tree nor plant grew—an expanse of flat, barren land, at the end of which rose a pole of fire. We were all walking toward that pole, whispering when we spoke, not a raised voice among us. Even the children were silent, as they strode with the flock.

There was among us an old man, bald and bare-headed and leaning on an oak cane, walking slowly and surely, his eyes fixed unwavering on his target. *I know this man*, I thought.

He turned to me as though he had heard my thoughts. "Yes, from very long ago," he communicated without speaking.

"May I ask you a question?"

"Be my guest," his eyes said.

The man did not speak. His eyes, his looks, expressed what he wanted to say. He made you wish that you, too, could tear words off your tongue and close your lips.

"It is a simple question. Can you tell me where we are going?"

His eyes moved and I understood that he meant the burning pole.

"Aren't we afraid of being burned?"

He turned away from me and gazed back at his distant goal.

A strange fear settled on my chest, and I felt a shiver run through my veins. The old man seemed to be the most alert of all, yet he rejected me.

I was lifted from my fear by the eyes of a child. His sweet face was turned towards me as he lay his head on his mother's shoulder. She walked, slightly stooped by his weight. She was tall and slim, and her chestnut hair fell around her shoulders, bouncing with every step she took.

"Where are we going?" I asked the child. His hazel eyes smiled at me and his tongue wagged with baby talk, "Goo, gaa ..."

"Are you serious?" I smiled back.

"Mama ... Baba ... Goo ... Gaa ..." And he ended his little conversation with a shy smile, burying his face in his mother's neck.

I went on with my silent walk and internal monologue. Suddenly a loud scream startled me, but it did not stop the others from marching. I turned, searching for the source of the scream, and found a woman lying on the ground as though resting.

"She is about to deliver," one person said.

"She needs help," another said.

"She can handle it on her own. We have no time to waste," admonished a third.

Their conversation was interrupted by another loud scream coming, it seemed, from the woman's very depths. And then I saw her roll herself together and hug herself as though trying to contain her pain. I tried to go near her when a giant hand appeared out of nowhere, suspended by invisible threads from somewhere between heaven and earth. I looked up to see where it had come from but it began to fade, slowly becoming transparent and disappearing.

"But she is ..."

"That is alright. Keep on walking." An unknown voice silenced the last of my protests.

I walked a few paces, my conscience nagging, then I turned around again. The woman had become but a dot on the distant horizon. I have not gone that far, I thought. I've only gone a few paces, yet the pregnant woman is now a distant point, forgotten. I looked around to draw someone's attention, but the pack had already traversed a long distance, leaving me behind.

My insides trembled. "And now what? What do I do?" My scream reverberated and echoed around the empty place, then came back to me, *What ... What ... What ...*

"This is impossible."

Impossible ... Impossible ... the echo returned.

"I have to run. I have to race the wind to catch up with them," I said silently, for fear of the echo.

I began to run, digging into my memory for the techniques I had used as a teenager when we used to race across the village. In that ancient time I was the fastest runner, always the winner at the competitions. I would arrive at the edge of the valley, under the large oak, and wait in ecstasy for my friends to appear at the finish line. I would hear their panting before I saw them. Then I would see the sparkle in their eyes and blood in their cheeks. My ecstasy would reach its height when they fell to the ground clutching at their knees in pain. Today I feel embarrassment, remembering my rapture at winning. The euphoria would pass through my veins and into my head, expanding it until it nearly touched the clouds.

"You cheat!"

"At running?" I would answer, mocking, indifferent.

"Yes!" They would shout in unison. "There is a secret, there must be a secret. No more competitions until we find out what the secret is." Then they would leave and I would remain alone wondering what the secret could be.

And now here I was, alone. The rest had gone ahead of me. I tried to remember what the secret was.

Lift your arms. A voice pierced the emptiness and ordered me. *Lift your arms and align them with your shoulders.*

I obeyed.

The voice continued, *Move them like a bird moves its wings.*

I did.

Stand on your toes.

I continued to obey blindly.

And now go ...

Memory launched me and I leapt over rooftops, over valleys and hills, past rivers and farmers. I soared through the air like an eagle, like a jet. I landed on the eaves of a roof. Our old clay roof. Suddenly the clay turned to hay and my feet started slipping ... slipping and I fell before I could remember to raise my arms and move them like wings. My fall awakened me and I opened my eyes, calming the trembling of my heart. I tried to assess the height from which I had fallen.

Here in this place there were no highs or lows. The land was flat and I was standing in the middle of nowhere, between an indistinct spot on the horizon and a human lump, racing the wind to reach a goal, a burning pole.

"It is the fire that lures you, can't you see?" My question, like a dart, rose out of me, hoping to spear a listener who would turn around and see me.

"The fire will burn you, don't you know that?" My voice travelled on the wind, and I heard its echo, but no one turned to me. Suddenly a face rose from the earth. A face I had not looked for: a white, oval, beady-eyed face, and a tongue that vibrated, emitting white foam.

"What? You here?"

The tongue vibrated, the eyes smiled, and the smile spread across the entire face, and then to the soft, luminous body.

"Where did you come from? You're the last person I expected to see at this moment," I said.

"You shouldn't forget," she answered.

"There has been some mistake. They linked our names together by mistake. I did not meet you. I was never under the tree and I never met you ... I had thought of taking a walk around the orchard and then you appeared from the other side. You were standing as you are now, stepping on your tail and smiling. And I was alone. I went out for a walk among the trees and green fields. Yes, I did speak to you, but only after you had spoken to me first. I was anxious to speak to anyone, any creature. I had a quarrel with the man, my partner, and I was looking for a sympathetic ear to listen to my complaints."

"Exactly, that is how I remember it," she said.

"You took advantage of the situation, of my weakness."

"I approached you offering my friendship and advice. Don't you remember?"

"And because of you I was punished. Thanks to your advice and your guidance we were both kicked out of Paradise. Because of you we lived in misery, eating, by the sweat of our brow, black, unleavened bread."

"That is because you did not hear what was first spoken."

"No, get away from me. I have no interest in hearing the spoken or the unspoken words."

"But you will ..."

"Who will force me to? You? You no longer frighten me."

"Fear will set in after I leave."

"What do you mean?"

"Think a little and you will know what I mean. Think fast and decide."

"I want no advice from you. Go back to where you came from. Leave me."

"You are left here until the end of time."

"How malicious!" I said as I rubbed my eyes, disbelieving. For hundreds of years I have been trying to wash out the traces of her ancient hissing, stuck in my ears like glue.

For thousands of years the glue adheres more tenaciously and spreads over my skin, into my pores.

Malicious! She chooses the worst moments, when the soul is ready to fall into sin. No ... I have learned my lesson. I will not let her in.

She tried to help you, said the unknown voice. *She lives alone here. This field is her playground, she romps and frolics here, without sentry or guard. You were the one who tread on her land. You are still trespassing on her soil. She can do with you as she pleases.*

"For instance?"

Take action against you.

"In a court?"

No, no. She doesn't need a court. She'll block your way.

"I was already in despair before she arrived on the scene."

She wanted to help you out of your despair.

"At what price?"

You did not give her a chance. You did not leave a door open for her.

I was left, abandoned in this desolate space, my friends moving, undaunted, towards their journey's goal—to reach the fiery pole, which was growing taller.

They moved towards it with lightning speed. I could see them from afar, a mass, round as a sphere, looking very much like the earth would from outer space. And like a ball rolls, they rolled toward the fire. My screams no longer reached them.

A few more steps and they would crash into the pole: the bald old man, the mother and child, the young men and women; all those who rose with the dawn, and with great enthusiasm decided to make this journey. In a little while they would reach their goal.

I was torn apart, suffocating, standing like a cactus tree in the desert, fruitless and barren. I lifted my arms and waited for the voice to penetrate the emptiness and come to me anew, with new instructions—that I might blindly obey.

The Lost Flour Mill

I recall the road well. Its paths and lanes, fenced by pomegranate and quince trees and bushes of wild berries, are etched in my memory. It swerves towards the mountain slope, slanting downward into the valley, where the waters from the river gush, fast and high.

The river runs between the forests of cane and reed, bypassing the proud poplars, the haughty sycamores and the reticent willows, until it reaches a tree unique among those of the valley. This tree sprawls, spreading its shade like a mother eager to embrace the universe. It spreads its fragrance over the area and from its bosom hang the fruits of its bounty—green in the early summer, ripening in September, tempting the children to pick them and pelt each other with them. The walnut tree! It shaded the old flour mill as though protecting a timid virgin from curious eyes.

As time went by, the old mill became more retiring and the walnut tree more protective; its roots digging tenaciously into the earth, its tops waving resolutely at the open spaces.

It was at a young age, now deeply rooted in the past, when my father decided to lease the flour mill and manage it himself, providing a service to the farmers and producing unadulterated flour and seed and grain whose very names stirred the appetite.

I still do not know why my father gave up tilling his land for that year, why he no longer planted and tended his crop of olive and grape and took on the flour mill instead. But I do know the seeds planted in my memory that year will last me a lifetime.

I moved from village life, sharply defined by the changing of the seasons and propelled by the pace of the farmers' footfalls, to a land of wonderment and revelation.

Each person coming to the mill carried a story. No sooner would they begin the first words than we, the children, would sit obediently on the narrow threshold, forgetting our mischief and playfulness to listen.

We were told long stories, in time to the strains of the millstone and the gurgle of the water as it rushed out through the opening in the mill, announcing unequivocally that it had finished its work and was returning to the river.

The good farmers' stories were flavoured with their lives and that of their villages—stories that started out true but strayed, in the telling, into the world of fantasy.

What more of life could a child of seven ask for, than to grow up with nature as her school? Once the pouch full of stories was depleted, we moved on, my siblings and I, riding the saddle of adventure. We climbed the trees at the edge of the precipice, where the slightest wrong move would have thrown us into the valley. We chased insects and reptiles, not differentiating between friend and foe. And once we were through exploring the outer layers of the soil, we dug deep into the belly of mother earth to discover what seeds and roots lay within its folds.

That was the world of my daytime. A world of continuous movement and surprise. As night fell, spreading darkness over the river banks and blanketing the trees, as the leaves whispered gently to the night and closed their sleepy lids, I moved into the exalted world of imagination. Every echo became the door to an unknown world I was eager to open. Each ray of light sparkling into the darkness, carried with it the promise of a distant planet. Every flutter of a night bird's wings opened a vein of ecstasy to my heart.

How I loved the night! I waited for it, preparing myself for its arrival in the hut my father had built for me on the roof of the flour mill. It was made of wooden planks and tree boughs, with straw mats for a floor, and peepholes in the corners for eyes that cannot wait to watch the dawn rise. Huddled in my hut, I felt as though I were sitting on top of a throne prepared for me by angels that sat around me, protecting me, providing for my happiness and comfort.

The year passed, the days falling off like pages from a calendar. One year followed another and the child became a woman, her land of dreams no more than a distant memory.

On an autumn day held captive by a bored sun, she would accompany her daughter to that distant valley. She had promised her daughter she would leave the city. They would leave behind the strangled, broken communication lines, the roads that were no longer roads, the homes haunted by echoes of days gone by, their small alcoves left standing to register their censure.

She had promised to take a day away from the life that had her turning in place like a beast of burden tied to a waterwheel. Except that she wasn't really turning. It was her world that turned while she submitted to the will of others.

Those others who had imposed war on her country, who had levelled her home and displaced her children, who had stolen the sleep from her eyes and stripped her of dreams and worldly pleasures.

She also submitted to the will of every workman and labourer, who carried his tools and trampled through her house (after it had lost the protectiveness of windows and doors), to bang a nail into a wall and promise the house would look like new.

She would take a vacation from work and weariness and the endless wait; from the monotony, the fear and the anxiety … from tomorrows and yesterdays; from the news and newspapers, the radio and the television; from foreign correspondents and politicians and special envoys; and from all those concerned parties who had dug the graves of their people.

"Yes," she had said. "Today I'll take a day off with my daughter. One day will neither advance nor hinder the course of my life."

In the car she took her place in the passenger seat next to her daughter. She surrendered to her musings, lost in thoughts that confused past, present and future in her mind.

She knew this day would create changes. It would awaken memories covered by the ashes of years, distorted by the fires of war.

"If it weren't for you, no one would have been able to forcibly remove me from my home and take me there again," she said to her daughter.

"Why are you so apprehensive about this trip?" the young woman asked. "The roads leading there are safe."

"I am afraid, child, of the sharp daggers of my memory." But she knew she would not be able to explain to her daughter what her words meant. It was a "business" trip, besides. Her daughter was preparing a study on ancient mills and factories (the old flour mill was one of them) and had decided to take advantage of her mother's association with that old world.

"Yes, dear," she had told her daughter, "the old mill is still there, standing at the neck of the river, the water gurgling past it to rapidly reach the end of its journey."

Now she said, "Stop the car here, where the paved road surrenders to the country lane. Let us continue on foot."

She did not wait for an answer. The minute her feet

touched the red earth of the valley of bounty, she did not look back. She nearly forgot her daughter and the purpose of the trip.

She was a child of six or seven once more. The orchards stretched out in front of her, the trees tempted her with their honeyed fruit. Bunches of gold and ruby grapes dangled from the vines like healthy pink cheeks and open smiling faces. The leaves on the trees flapped like birds' wings, inviting her, whispering words of welcome to her. She heard voices rising from the depth of the valley—the voices of happy children with no restrictions and no curfews. She could almost see them, running barefoot, their tiny feet blistered and red with droplets of blood. Ah, but what mattered was the rosiness of their cheeks.

Those were her childhood friends. With them she ran those orchards tens of times. She knew every corner and every pathway. She knew where the branches were thickest, where they intermingled and huddled as though in secret conference, where they bent towards the river, imparting their secret to the waters.

She knew the forests and the streams, the bird nests and the havens where the cattle lay to rest. Today her daughter had given her the opportunity to recall all that.

She ran as though a thousand hands were pushing her, carrying her, oblivious of the thorns and the pebbles in her path. She ran, never once looking back. She could see the past in front of her, opening a path to the future.

The road guided her and she did not slow down. She knew it would lead her to the old mill, and the walnut tree where she would finally come to rest.

"I think we're lost."

It was her daughter's voice that brought her back to the present. It was discordant somehow, unrelated to what she saw around her and what she felt. Instinctively she needed to defend herself, defend her place and her past, "I am sure the old mill is over there, behind that orchard."

"You mean it *used* to be there." The young woman laughed.

"And what used to be still is."

"This will always be a point of contention between us, dear Mother. You will not admit that a place may change. Sometimes even cease to exist totally."

"But the mill ... the river ..."

"Only in memory, Mother, within the depths of your roots that hold tenaciously to this land."

"Let me just walk a few more steps." She pleaded with her daughter, but she had lost all confidence and her words lacked certainty.

Suddenly she realized that the road she had chosen was no longer a road. It had become part of the orchard trees, which hugged and huddled like the members of a close family.

She turned around, looking for the walnut tree, to use it as a landmark, a sign. And she was shocked to find dozens of trees strewn all around the field. Not one of them bent lovingly over an old flour mill.

She walked away with her daughter, her head bent, dragging her feet, tripping over her desolation. She only saw the jagged-edged stone as she stumbled on it. A strangled cry escaped her and she would have fallen had her daughter not supported her.

It was the millstone.

She was standing atop the ruins of her cherished flour mill—and here it was buried, under the layers of earth and years.

They Are All His Mother

" **W**ho is the woman sitting on the doorstep, cloaked in ageless misery?"

"That, my friend, is his mother."

"And the other one, next to her, garbed in black?"

"His mother."

"What of that one ... and that ... and that?"

"All of them ... they are all his mother."

∞

This is not a passage from a Greek tragedy, but the introduction to the story I will relate to you. It happened yesterday and today, and it will recur tomorrow. And if time and place should change, the events will remain the same. And no sooner should a protagonist fall than he will be replaced by another, for the show must go on and the audience waits, rapt and breathless.

In this story, I alone was the audience. The rest had gone up to the stage to take their designated places and perform their assigned roles.

I stood in the middle of the theatre, confused at the action taking place and the scenes unfolding around me.

I was unaware of my own self. All I could hear and see were exploding scenes and deafening cries. In my daze I did not know where to look or what to look at—and all the while, events of the past echoed through my mind.

In shadowy corners, my eyes met unfamiliar ghosts wearing masks. Intuitively I was able to discern the identities of those behind the masks, but I held my peace.

My silence lengthened as the cries around me grew wilder, pervading the world, falling like rain and rising to the heavens.

Cries and their echoes were the only means of expression. I listened closely, trying to catch a word or two amid the screams, but could not. I only heard screams.

My eagerness for knowledge grew and I wanted to understand what was happening on that stage: what were they doing, what were they saying?

Clearly, no one had any intention of answering my question or responding to my wishes. They were all too busy emitting their horrific screams. And whereas at the beginning I could tell the characters apart, I could no longer do that now. They had merged together into a solid mass of human forms whose only aim was to cry and howl.

I stepped back and looked around me. I attempted to get assistance from the masked forms lurking in the corners but they, too, ignored me.

"I want to understand what is going on. I am your only audience."

My plea echoed around and returned to me unanswered.

"Am I the only ignorant stranger in this place?"

Once again I heard no answer, but I was not deterred from continuing my monologue.

"Tell me, do you want me to leave here? I am your only audience."

Still no one answered me.

"Dear God ..." I released a supplication, to prevent despair from engulfing me. "These people don't care for my presence. Why then am I here?" I would leave at once, I decided, and began looking for an exit. But I found no exit signs anywhere. I would have to stay in the theatre, and maybe perish listening to the screams and howls explode around me.

In my despair I did not notice that one spectre had removed its mask and approached me. "How long have you been here?" it asked.

"From the start. From when the curtain came up," I answered, with some trepidation.

"What have you seen? What have you understood?"

I hung my head in shame. "The truth is I have understood nothing, for I am accustomed to a dialogue of words."

"And they are screaming."

"That's right, that's right," I said with great relief. Here at last was someone who understood my predicament and might be able to rescue me.

"Why do you stay?"

My despair returned. "There are no exits and the passage ways are blocked. It seems I am destined to remain here."

The spectre nodded. But instead of the explanation I had hoped for, the spectre replaced his mask and turned away from me, returning to his assigned place.

My hopefulness was shortlived. The spectre's retreat plunged me into deeper despair. There was no way out for me. I returned to watch the characters and their eerie howls.

A woman shrouded in black detached herself from the human mass and approached the centre of the stage. It was her voice that gave her away as a woman, for she was swathed in black from head to toe. Her shrill voice tore out of her lungs and filled the atmosphere with anguish and dread.

"She is mourning her child ..." a voice from nowhere informed me.

A clearer picture began to form in my mind. I now understood that the woman had lost her child, which explained her black garb, her grief, her ghastly howls and eerie screams. But what about all the others?

Another body detached itself from the human mass and joined the woman centre stage. The two bodies held each other and emitted one heart-rending scream.

"That is the child's father," the voice explained again.

As long as I maintained a connection with this voice I would not be totally lost, I thought, whether it is the voice of my subconscious or an other-world voice.

Despite the black mood around me, some of my hope returned. The mist was lifting by virtue of this guiding voice. And I was able to share these people's sorrow. Warm tears rolled down my face and sank into the earth.

"I am crying. Watering the earth beneath me with my tears."

"But you are not his mother," the voice admonished.

"But I am a mother," I replied, able at last to speak confidently to the voice.

"Your tears remain offstage. Remember you are only the audience."

"But I am a participating audience," I answered, proud of my courage, and the voice was silent. I wondered whether it had left me to follow the action alone.

Turning back to the stage, I saw mothers' forms repeatedly detach themselves from the crowd—once, twice, then three times. The multiple mothers formed a circle and the others in the circle became their centre.

"This is a very important part of the action. Watch closely. Do you see any difference between them?" The voice spoke again.

I nearly answered affirmatively, but decided I was too hasty. I should observe them before making any comment. After careful scrutiny I could see no difference between one woman and the other. They were identical in shape and form, in height and size, in clothes.

"They are all his mother," I said.

I understood that intuitively, but intellectually I failed

to understand how one child could have this many mothers. I had not yet spoken the thought when the voice anticipated it.

"It is very simple," it said.

"How is that? I don't understand."

"Ask your tears."

"My tears are outsiders. The audience's tears."

"The participating audience," it reminded me, compassionately. "All barriers between the audience and the actors have been removed."

No sooner had the voice finished speaking than the first mother broke the circle and walked blindly to edge of the stage. My heart lurched. I was sure she would fall, for she walked like someone entranced. I closed my eyes and waited to hear the thud of her body hit the ground. When it did not come, I peeked furtively, like a child cheating at a game of hide-and-seek. She had crossed some invisible line and was continuing her ghostly walk towards me.

I trembled, frightened. I had not anticipated that I would come face to face with her. I had been a spectator, an auditor. I was an outsider and here she was approaching me. Her hands, white as snow against the folds of her black garb and glowing with a strange light, were extended towards me.

I opened my eyes, all my senses keen, pulling myself together to face her fearlessly. She continued to approach and her black cloak was no longer clear, and her arms emitted a strange unearthly light.

"Come ..." her voice whispered.

"Give me your hands ... only your hands."

I extended my hands to her, anxiety racking me. "What may I do for you?"

"Just give me your hands ..."

I extended both hands again. I was suddenly ready to put my whole being at her disposal, without questioning her intentions. But she turned away and went back to the stage. She did not even touch my hands. She had been testing me.

As soon as she returned to the circle, each of the forms I had perceived as women detached themselves from the mass and became individual entities. Then they were suddenly transformed into a giant tree, scraping the ceiling and seeming to go through it into space.

"This is a new act," my mentor-voice explained, lifting me out of my ignorance. "A new act worthy of your attention."

"But I don't understand."

"That's alright. The important thing is that you remain here."

"But how do you explain the transformation I witnessed. It is beyond human comprehension."

The voice laughed, mocking me. "Is that the only thing you find beyond human comprehension? Oh, but you are naive."

How dare he scold me? I thought angrily. How dare he call me naive when all I wanted was to understand what was happening? I had entered this place to learn.

"Don't you understand, you arrogant, conceited Voice, I am here to learn, to understand. Is this the theatre of the absurd?"

"Certainly not. It is the theatre of the rational."

"Rational? A mother becomes a tree?"

"With its roots firmly in the earth."

"Allegorically, symbolically, yes. But I am seeing it happen in reality."

"She did that to save herself."

"From what?"

"From annihilation, extinction. Do you wish to trace the path her roots have taken?"

"Into the earth's depths, you mean?"

"Yes. You could, if you tried, see them spreading through those black depths, going through the grains of the soil, absorbing the moisture and coldness, plunging deeper, searching in the darkness for what they were unable to find in the light."

"Then the transformation is not futile?"

"It has a vital purpose. Look, watch the roots spread, unravel the components of which the secrets of the earth are made, returning them to their primal state and seeking out that organism with which they wish to unite."

"The living organism?"

"Yes. The one living organism they had brought forth into the world. Do you understand now the secret of that transformation you witnessed on stage? Do you understand its purpose?"

"Perhaps ..." I said uncertainly.

"You need time. Time for meditation and tranquillity."

At that point, the voice abandoned me in the hall of the theatre, which had now been transformed into a forest of wild and unusual trees whose roots were seeking to unite with the one living organism they had spawned, while their heads extended into the clouds.

Lost in my confusion, I heard a rustling sound in the emptiness around me. I looked around to the spectres that had been hiding in the corners. I hoped they would provide me with further explanations. I hoped they would dissipate the mist that blurred my vision. Instead I watched as they retreated into the hidden corners, closing doors behind them. Walls rose in front of them. There was nothing left.

∞

Let me assure you once again, before I leave this theatre, that what I have just related is not a passage from a Greek tragedy. It is merely part of a story.

The story began yesterday. It continues today, and it may recur tomorrow.

This terrifies me, but I know that it may recur.

A Miracle

Carried upon a cloud, she floated, and with her were her three little quails, Samer, Leila and Nadim. Her feet touched the earth, the sky was a hat she wore with pride. The rays of the golden June sun filtered through her hair.

The trees leaned one against the other, their branches downcast in sadness and confusion. Why were they sad when the chirping of birds filled the air? Where had all those colourful chirping birds come from, she wondered? Perhaps the jinn were celebrating a summer wedding around the city.

The city opened its arms to her, embraced her, opened its streets so she could better move along them. The city today was as she had never known it before. It looked like an abstract painting of flat lands out of which rose buildings whose windows and doors were shuttered against the sun. And the sun that morning was heavy in the sky, like a body weighted down by fatigue. Her youngest, Nadim, could paint pictures like this one.

She pressed his hand in hers and he tucked his face into the folds of her dress for protection.

Leila asked, "Where have all the people gone, Mama? The people we used to meet on the streets."

She answered guardedly, "They may have gone to the wedding."

"Whose wedding?" inquired Leila.

Her mother answered, her eyes on a body that slashed across the sky like lightning. "The wedding of the jinn."

Leila was silent, as though she did not understand. Or maybe she understood more than she should have. Samer interrupted, explaining to his sister and pointing towards the foreign object in the sky, "It's a rocket."

"That is one of the jinn birds. Did I not tell you the story about the jinn?" said their mother.

Nadim felt a lightness in his chest at the words, and insisted with all the innocence of his five years that his mother tell him the story of where this bird came from.

His mother squeezed his hand again and bent towards him to place a comforting kiss on his forehead. "I will tell you later."

The four continued on their way, taken by what they saw and did not see.

∞

An hour before, Souad had knocked on the door of her home. The home of which she had been mistress at one time—four years ago to be precise. She had shared a good and tranquil and love-filled life with her man. That was before she had been struck down and lost consciousness. After that, and after she had been examined by doctors, it was determined that she had lost her mental balance.

She remained under treatment for a long time, and remained beyond the realm of the rational. Her body was healthy—the defect lay hidden somewhere within folds of the grey matter. She had days of clarity and brightness when she would be normal again; and those close to her could forget about her mental disorder. But then she would return to the bottomless abyss of psychological and mental torment. She would scream and trash anything she got her hands on, not sparing herself.

Her husband had tried to adapt to the situation. He tried to help her. He made a myriad of efforts. But the problem was more than he could deal with, and it nearly swept away their home and their children, the eldest of whom had been four at the time.

The doctors had released their verdict on Souad's condition, and therefore the sentence on the entire family: Souad must be institutionalized. The rest would be left to the will of God.

But the miracle did not happen.

Souad remained at the institution for four years. Her condition was normal as long as she was within familiar surroundings—in her room, the grounds, her doctor's clinic. But when she moved away from the tranquil surroundings it was anybody's guess what could happen.

A year ago the doctor had allowed her weekend visits at home. He had hoped she would gradually return to her normal life.

Her husband made every effort to make her stay comfortable and enjoyable, and beneficial to both mother and children. He had also hired a strong and capable nanny to care for the children and see to their needs.

For an entire year nothing marred the peacefulness of the family. Everyone became accustomed to the new routine. The children considered that they now had two mothers, one who lived with them, fed and clothed them and saw to their needs, and another who visited on weekends and holidays.

When Leila told her father of this he seemed pleased at the thought, yet saddened by it. "Blessed are the children," he said to himself and wished he possessed Leila's innocence and ability to accept the circumstances.

∞

Today was not a weekend, yet Souad had come to visit the children. She did not ask about her husband. He had been away on business for weeks, and the children were home, forced to remain behind closed doors, being taken care of by their other "mother."

Samer, the eldest, opened the door, and his mother pounced on him to kiss and embrace him tightly, nearly choking the air out of him, as though attempting to make up for days of deprivation.

Leila arrived, skipping on one foot and singing, "Mama, Mama! Mama's here!" She was followed by Nadim. Souad took all three into her embrace. The nanny stood in the hallway watching the scene, unable to believe that the woman had actually gone out on a day like today, when even the birds were silent and all movement was at a standstill in the city.

To convince herself of the reality of what she was witnessing she asked, "How were you able to get here, Madam Souad?"

Souad answered with a smile. The same smile she had given her nurse, who had tried to stop her from leaving the institution. She had merely smiled. She could see, as though from far away, the faces of her little ones, as bright as crystal, shining like stars. Their eyes had called to her.

The nanny repeated her question. "Are the roads safe?" she added.

"I am here now, among you. And I miss my children," Souad answered her.

Singing, the children took her into their room. The windows were closed and the curtains drawn. Samer told her of Nanny's orders. Since their father had been away they had not left the house. He was away to deal with his business, and the unrest had begun only two days after he left. The neighbourhood had suddenly erupted in flame and the sky rained bullets and thick black clouds choked everything.

Souad listened to Samer as though hearing a voice that had travelled centuries to reach her, then she approached the windows, drew back the curtains and said, "Let the sun in ... The sun is our friend and carries goodness."

The children were silent, not knowing what to do. Nanny's directions were clear and indisputable: "We do not open the windows or doors. We do not go out on the balconies. We do not look out of the window. When we hear bullets fired we run to the inner corridor of the house. And when the bullets become explosions, we go down into the shelter with the rest of the neighbours."

They knew very well what to do. The nanny had been repeating instructions to them for ten days. She would start as soon as the sun rose.

Their father had not been able to return. He could, however, call them on the telephone. His phone calls were their only link to true safety. His voice gave them faith. His calls, always in the evening, made the coming night easier to endure.

And now here was their mother. And she had defied all the rules and broken all the laws. They felt as though she was with them, on their side, protesting. But Samer spoke up for all of them saying, "Mother Ratiba does not allow that."

His mother did not seem to have heard him and continued to express her own train of thoughts, "What do you say we go out for a walk."

Leila opened her mouth to protest but Samer clamped his hand over it and complimented the idea. "Great idea. As long as we don't tell Mother Ratiba." He spoke in whispers, taking his mother's hand and walking carefully into the corridor. Leila and Nadim walked behind them. Samer, the little rascal, did not forget to leave the radio playing loud jazz music to cover their escape.

When the nanny came to check on the children she felt instinctively that human warmth had left the house. She opened the door to their room and stood at the threshold, stunned by the open curtains and windows. The main door to the outside was open...sun and light poured in. Where were the children?

When she could not find them on the balcony, she was overcome by a fear that left her limp. A dark thought occurred to her: had Souad been overcome by one of her fits? Had she thrown herself and her children off the balcony?

She looked at the street below but saw no trace of anyone. Bullets whizzed by, assaulting her senses, robbing her of all ability to think clearly and move efficiently.

She ran to the outer door and tumbled down the stairs, shouting: Samer, Leila, Nadim ... The only answer was the sporadic ululation of gun-fire coming from the opposite side of the street. In her confusion she lost all thought of what to do next. On impulse she knocked on the neighbour's door. The only answer she received was, "Who would dare go out under this hail of fire?"

She went back into her home, sat and wept, preparing herself for more tears of recrimination, sadness and sorrow.

She did not know how much time had passed as she sat in silence and tears, submerged in a sea of fear and mental distraction.

What would she tell their father when he called and asked to speak to his children, as he did every evening? What could she tell him? How should she handle this? The questions descended upon her like bullets and doubts pierced her soul to the quick. Her heart beat faster with every explosion that echoed from outside. She wished this beating heart would stop so that she could be at peace. She could not take anymore of this ... she was bereft.

She wanted to call on someone for help, but all she found surrounding her were silent walls and an inane emptiness. She tried to recoup her strength, her faith. She tried to repeat her prayer for troubled times, but her tongue was tied in knots and her memory stretched like an arid, barren desert. Her memory had become a blank wall with no outlets.

She closed her eyes and fell asleep in her chair by the front door. She slept as one who never wanted to awaken, and dreamed of strange occurrences. She saw children running, chased by fire; children on their mother's arms, their faces wearing masks of horror; men and women, weak and elderly, piled atop one another, crying and screaming, and a universe split open like the mouth of an abyss. No one answered their screams. No one answered. She tried to reach out to the weak ones. She tried to save the children and carry them to safety away from the devouring fire. She tried to rise from her place and go to their rescue, but her chair had turned into a magnetic field, it drew her and held her in place.

Her chair was still holding on to her when the explosion echoed through the air. She saw a scarlet hole in the sky spewing flame.

Hours later, when she woke, she looked around her. All colour had faded to become one, the essence of all other colours. She opened her mouth to speak, to ask, but a young woman in white standing next to her clamped it shut for her. The woman whispered to her gently, "Praise God for your safety. It was the greatest miracle."

I Pretend

I pretend I am walking. And I walk. I pretend the sun is shining upon my house, and spring has filled my garden with light. I open my windows and my doors and I welcome the new day.

I look for the birds and I pretend that I hear them chirping to the rising dawn, as they land on my window sill to nibble on the crumbs as they have always done. As they did long ago, when my garden was fenced with trees. They squabble and quarrel as they feed, and their querrulous noises awaken the joy in me.

I pretend the pummeling on the wall is the flapping of their wings and not snipers' bullets gone astray. I pretend the wide street in front of my house is still a wide street, quiet and welcoming. I pretend that it still connects me to other streets in the city like a giant artery, keeping the circulation going.

I walk over the sidewalks as I have always walked, and I pretend the roadblock in my way is but a figment of my imagination, for I have just come from the land of slumber. My mind is enveloped in the night's fog, and the night's humidity forms a lingering mist that obstructs my view. I make a slight detour to avoid the barricade. I tell my cowering soul that I did not really bump into a powder keg, nor did I step on the barbed wire that encircles the streets, the sidewalks and the pathways—and clutches at my heart.

I bend, I stand up straight. My head is held high, my eyes focusing straight ahead of me. I do not see the hole in the ground, gaping like an evil eye, and murky with foul water. I fall into it. My foot sinks into its depth and the pugnacious stench assaults my senses. Gingerly I extract my foot and continue on my way.

I pretend the sound of explosions that invades my thoughts and shakes the wall against which I lean is nothing but overzealous celebrations. I pretend, too, that the pressure that kicked my brain, glued me to my place, then threw me across the room, was nothing but a passing inconvenience. I am alright. Thank God. I am in one piece, I have not lost any part of my body nor any of my senses. So, my heart has accelerated frighteningly, my blood pressure has risen astronomically, my throat and mouth are parched, my arms and legs are numb and my fingers and toes are ice cold ... It doesn't matter, these are symptoms that come with living in Beirut, as fear comes with living in a jungle.

And I pretend. I pretend my inner capacity for love has not yet dried up and its source and nurturer is not gone. I engulf it with my wings and get ready to soar, for I long to see you. I dream that we will meet again, on some road, by some twist of fate. You have been gone so long and my longing for you boils within my veins and overflows while all around me spreads the coldness of death. You had accustomed me to the warmth and intimacy of your presence.

I pretend that deep inside of me still flow the juices of our old love, dripping into my soul, feeding it, mending it, resuscitating it with their fragrance. I pretend that, should I lift my gaze from its resting place on the sand, or tear my eyes away from the sidewalk in front of me, I would see your face in all its glory and all its beauty, as I had known it. It was my daily bread. I stretch my arm. I stretch my arm to you and with it is all the longing in my soul. And without moving my lips, I ask you to take my fingers in your hands and rub them. With the strength of your gentleness you will drive away the coldness of death, the iciness that now resides permanently in them.

I pretend you are near me, you hear, see, understand and know, and that my feelings reach you and touch you. You extend a gentle hand to me from your faraway place and lift me from the depths of my despair. We walk together by the shore and listen to the waves break upon the rocks and hear the hysterical cries of the seagulls as they race and fight over trash floating on the water's surface. I pretend that from my heart rises a message to you, like steam rising from boiling liquid, to tell you it is not yet over and our time awaits, we shall meet again in love.

I pretend the war has not destroyed my inner fortifications, has not wiped out my words and butchered my feelings; has not separated us, scattered us, forced us to count days instead of living them, waiting to meet again.

And when we meet again, we'll pretend that we were never apart. We'll pretend that all the toil and hardship, the pain and hunger, the death, and all that we lived through and died of, was an illusion. We will pretend we have attained victory, and here we stand at the pinnacle of existence announcing it: our victory over despair and loss and death. We will rise from the ashes, new birds, reborn, contemporary descendants of that old phoenix.

I pretend my fingers touch your high forehead to make sure you are still there, you have not left me. I pretend my fingers are laced in yours, my arm around you as we walk, once more, along the beach. While you sing your songs to me, I look ahead and I see the happpiness that awaits me for all the days of my life. I pretend that your songs echo through my soul, rising toward the heavens, drowning out the deafening explosions and the cries of bereaved mothers.

I pretend the long war that has dried the grass and stomped upon our souls has not achieved its goal, that all the fire and destruction have not killed the seeds of hope buried in the depths of the earth. I pretend that the collapse of what we had built with pride, was but a winter's nightmare. I pretend that the essence of what we built remains, will always live, and that the seeds we planted will grow for we still believe in our tomorrows and in humankind and in perseverence. I pretend the storm has not uprooted us, for the fences we built with the light of our eyes were stronger. And the storm with all its force was still powerless to uproot the evergreens and the palm trees. It was only capable of drying up some moss and weeds, and passing on to oblivion. And the trees have once again risen to embrace one another and sway in space.

I pretend we will walk out into the sunshine, into our little garden, and sit on its green benches and drink our cardamom-flavoured coffee and listen to the twittering and quarrelling of birds high up in the old oak and greet our old friends. I pretend we will rise again to face another day, a new day.

I pretend our precious home, rising on the mountaintop like an eagle's nest, has not been demolished, nor have its very foundations been destroyed. It remains, and in it remains the smell of our children, the sound of their laughter, the pictures of their smiling faces and handfuls of intimacy, familiarity and mirth.

I pretend our home in the city also awaits friends and loved ones, its doors and windows open, unaware of those who would pounce on it, and destroy it.

I pretend all is as it used to be: people peaceful and loving; children being born, birds and butterflies hatching; flowers blossoming in the fields, on balconies and window sills. I pretend the sun still rises and sets; the moon and the stars adorn the skies; the seasons still follow one after the other. I pretend the blue expanse that is sea and sky remains pure and clear, untarnished by the battleships in its midst, unsullied by enemy aggression. It is still our cover and our horizon, over which we row our little boats while we sing our songs of freedom.

I pretend you will return to the little nest we built together. The storms of change will not uproot us. You will return, your voice as strong as thunder, overriding other sounds of thunder that penetrate my slumber and turn my dreams to nightmares.

I pretend I am still young, a girl of but twenty, standing on her balcony, her heart trembling, her eyes shining with happiness, her lips yearning. Waiting, her arms impatient in their longing to hold you within their circle. And when you return, when the miracle happens and you return, descending like an eagle from the mountaintops—carrying with you the faces of those that the smoke of war has obliterated—I promise you I will ask forgiveness for all I said in your absence, while I sat wrapped in the mist. I promise you I will no longer pretend. I will believe in miracles and speak of my belief. And know this, my love, know that in our godless time, in this, the last quarter of our crooked century, at the dawning of a new one, in this age of deprivation, of violence and famine, of decadence, I will turn believer. In spite of all we see and do not see, all we hear and long to hear, in spite of all the pain and all the suffering there is still a place for miracles, if you return.

But until such a time, until the vision becomes reality, I will go on living in the mist, shrouded in fantasy. And I will pretend that I walk along my normal path among people who have not lost all feeling, or the essence of their being; among people who have not resigned from humanity, and have not yet despaired of arriving at it.

I pretend I am walking—and I walk, deaf to all sound and echo that might invade my world and my solitude. For if I don't, I will disappear.

ABOUT THE AUTHOR

EMILY NASRALLAH grew up in the small village of Kfeir, south Lebanon. The eldest of six children, she attended the American University of Lebanon in Beirut, where she became active as a journalist and writer. Her first novel, *Birds of September*, was published in 1962, and won her three Arabic literary prizes. It is now in its seventh edition. It was followed by five novels, one children's book, and five short story collections which explore themes such as family roots and the struggle of women for independence in a male-dominated country. Her commitment to feminism has resulted in the banning of two of her books in some Arab countries. She is one of a number of women Lebanese authors known as the Beirut Decentrists, who stayed in Beirut, shared the experience of the war and wrote about conflict from a woman's point of view.

Emily participated in the 1988 International Olympics Authors Festival in Calgary and was a panelist and guest reader at the 1989 PEN International Congress in Toronto and Montreal. She is a contributor to Miriam Cooke's *War's Other Voices: Women Writers on the Lebanese Civil Wars* (Cambridge University Press).

Her novel, *Flight Against Time*, was published in English in 1987 by Ragweed Press. Married, with four children, Emily divides her time between Beirut, Cairo and Canada.

ABOUT THE TRANSLATOR

THURAYA KHALIL-KHOURI is a freelance editor and translator living in Toronto. She studied English literature at the American University of Beirut and has taught English as a second language in the Middle East and Europe. Since coming to Canada, Ms. Khalil-Khouri has worked on a number of translation and editorial projects including editing and producing *The Arab Canadian*, the newsletter of the Canadian Arab Federation. She has also spoken at a number of conferences and radio shows representing the Arab-Canadian community in Toronto.

Ms. Khalil-Khouri is fluent in three languages. She occasionally writes and interprets.

A House Not Her Own in her first major translation work.

THE BEST OF gynergy books

∞ **A House Not Her Own: Stories from Beirut,** *Emily Nasrallah.* In seventeen powerful and poetic stories, internationally acclaimed Lebanese author and feminist Emily Nasrallah writes about what she knows only too well: war. But these are the stories that are rarely told—of the civilians who live within the bombed-out shell of Beirut, who try to recreate a past through memories, even as the landmarks and monuments of that past are destroyed. ISBN 0-921881-19-3 $ 12.95

∞ **By Word of Mouth: Lesbians write the erotic,** *Lee Fleming (ed.).* A bedside book of short fiction and poetry by thirty-one lesbian writers from Canada and the United States. ISBN 0-921881-06-1 $ 10.95 / $ 12.95 US

∞ **Don't: A Woman's Word,** *Elly Danica.* The best-selling account of incest and recovery, both horrifying and hauntingly beautiful in its eventual triumph over the past. ISBN 0-921881-05-3 $ 8.95 (US rights held by Cleis Press)

∞ **Each Small Step: Breaking the chains of abuse and addiction,** *Marilyn MacKinnon (ed.).* This groundbreaking anthology contains personal narratives by women at various stages of recovery from the traumas of childhood sexual abuse and alcohol and chemical dependency. ISBN 0-921881-17-7 $ 10.95

∞ **Fascination and other bar stories,** *Jackie Manthorne.* These are satisfying stories of the rituals of seduction and sexuality in the otherworld of lesbian bars—fascinating fiction for lesbians. ISBN 0-921881-16-9 $ 9.95

∞ **Friends I Never Knew,** *Tanya Lester.* In this finely crafted novel, Tara exiles herself on an island to write about five extraordinary women she has known over the years in the women's movement. These women, speaking in the pages of her notebook, bring Tara out of exile and allow her the freedom to act one again. ISBN 0-921881-18-5 $ 10.95

∞ **getting wise,** *Marg Yeo.* Women-loving poems of resistance and triumph. Marg Yeo shares hard-won truths and "the fine delight there will always be for me in poems and women." ISBN 0-921881-13-4 $ 8.95 / $ 7.95 US

∞ **The Montreal Massacre,** *Marie Chalouh and Louise Malette (eds.).* Feminist letters, essays and poems examine the mass murder of fourteen women at Ecole Polytechnique in Montreal, Quebec on December 6, 1989. The writers express a common theme: the massacre was the extreme manifestation of misogyny in our patriarchal society. ISBN 0-921881-14-2 $ 12.95

∞ **Somebody Should Kiss You,** *Brenda Brooks.* An intimate, humorous and bold collection of poetry that celebrate the courage of lesbian lives and loves. ISBN 0-921881-12-6 $ 8.95/ $ 7.95 US

∞ **Sous la langue / Under Tongue,** *Nicole Brossard.* "Bound by a sensuous pale grey-green cover, the exquisite poetry within is about desire, the unforeseen, personal thoughts of anticipation, prolongation, suspension of making love. Brossard's language rolls under tongue, over tongue, around and around inside the body. Sensual. Erotic." *(f)/Lip* ISBN 0-921881-00-2 $ 15.00

∞ **Tide Lines: Stories of change by lesbians,** *Lee Fleming (ed.).* These diverse stories explore the many faces of change—instantaneous, over-a-lifetime, subtle or cataclysmic. ISBN 0-921881-15-0 $ 10.95

gynergy books is distributed in Canada by UTP, in the U.S. by Bookpeople and Inland and in the U.K. by Turnaround. Individual orders can be sent, prepaid, to: *gynergy books,* P.O. Box 2023, Charlottetown, PEI, Canada, C1A 7N7. Please add postage and handling ($1.50 for the first book and 75 cents for each additional book) to your order. Canadian residents add 7% GST to the total amount. GST registration number R104383120.